MATCHI

Mr James Jarvis, orthopaedic consultant at the Frantfield and General, is reputed to leave a trail of cast-off crutches, mended bones and broken hearts behind him. But, Nurse Hester Stanton vows, he will not get away with ruining her sister's life for a second time . . .

MATCHMAKER NURSE

BY

BETTY BEATY

MILLS & BOON LIMITED
London · Sydney · Toronto

First published in Great Britain 1984
by Mills & Boon Limited, 15–16 Brook's Mews,
London W1A 1DR

© Betty Beaty 1984

Australian copyright 1984
Philippine copyright 1984

ISBN 0 263 74648 8

Set in 12 on 12½ pt Linotron Times
03–0484–41,000

*Photoset by Rowland Phototypesetting Ltd
Bury St Edmunds, Suffolk
Made and printed in Great Britain by
Richard Clay (The Chaucer Press) Ltd
Bungay, Suffolk*

CHAPTER ONE

'NURSE! Nurse Stanton! Come over here! *At once!*'

The controlled anger in Sister's voice echoed through the mid-morning quiet of Bonnington ward where twenty sympathetic men, in various stages of orthopaedic injury, heard Sister round on one of the student nurses again.

In this case one of their favourites, Hester Stanton—a smiling eager twenty-year-old, who wore the white cap with the two thin blue stripes of a second-year student jauntily on her thick wavy brown hair, who was always willing to do the odd errand, and who frequently fell foul of Sister.

The fault was plainly Mick O'Rourke's at whose bed the surgical team was now gathered. He was the black sheep of the ward. But Sister was laying it on for the benefit of the new orthopaedic consultant, Mr James Jarvis, a tall, dark visaged man with the build of a Rugby forward, who was now beginning his first clinical round.

The patients of Bonnington had been curious to see this Mr Jarvis. He had been appointed very quickly because his predecessor had suffered a coronary, which was likely to incapacitate him for some time. Surprisingly young though Mr Jarvis was for the appointment, his reputation had spread before him here to the Frantfield and District Hospital. Mr Jarvis had spent some time as a houseman at the parent Fosse Memorial Hospital in London. He was an athlete, a keen climber and tough, Sister had told them all, even by orthopaedic standards. Everyone knew the qualities required for a good ortho-pod—strong steady hands, strong muscles, strong wills. Mr Jarvis was well endowed with all those qualities. Squeal and whimper as they might, no one would get the better of Mr Jarvis.

'When Mr Jarvis says you will walk the length of the ward and back, *you will walk*,' Sister had told them with unconcealed satisfaction, her boot-button eyes momentarily bright with admiration. 'And when Mr Jarvis says you can do without your Zimmer, back to Physio it goes. You won't get round Mr Jarvis. *No way*.'

Sister, short, plump and in her middle thirties, feared nothing and no one except of being got round. And since the admission to her ward of Mick O'Rourke, the show jumper, after a fall at Hickstead, Sister suspected that some of her nurses were being got round by his charming Irish ways. And even she, all formid-able five feet of energy and dedication, found some difficulty in maintaining her normal cast-iron discipline.

Despite a fractured clavicle, a fractured femur, two ribs and two toes, the irrepressible Irishman always found something to celebrate. Now he was intent on celebrating today as his twenty-first birthday, though his medical notes said plainly he was twelve years older than that last December, and he had a bottle of champagne half uncorked on the floor beside his bed to help him with the celebration.

'Sure, Sister,' Mick O'Rourke began as second-year student nurse Hester Stanton hurried over, 'An' you wouldn't be after denying a man on his birthday . . .' he tried blinking his wicked, thickly-lashed blue eyes, and smiled his lopsided practised smile.

'Sure, an' she would, I promise,' Mr Jarvis mocked him tersely. Then he looked at his wrist watch with some impatience.

'Pick up that bottle and get rid of it,' Sister hissed in Nurse Stanton's ear. 'Don't stand there staring!'

But Nurse Stanton still remained for a second rooted to the spot. She stared neither at the offending bottle, nor at the protesting patient, but at Mr Jarvis who stood on the other side of Sister, his hands thrust into the pockets of his white coat. Hester's golden brown eyes were wide, her full lips slightly parted. For a moment, Mr Jarvis' keen grey eyes met her own indignant stare. His eyes were uncomprehending and unrecognising as if he saw no more than an anonymous student nurse in her plain short-sleeved dress. Then she noticed his thick black brows draw together, and his lips tighten at what must seem her obtuseness. She had only seen this man once before, and then she had been very young. Less than ten years old. But he was not the kind of man even a child completely forgot.

'Nurse!' Sister gave her a light push forward.

Hester was suddenly galvanised into action. She bent down hastily and picked up the bottle in hands that still trembled with anger. Straightening she flicked one more hostile glance at Mr Jarvis. Now that face and name were together in her mind, she remembered it all.

James Jarvis at twenty-three, newly qualified, coming down from London for her sister Caroline's twenty-first birthday party. Caroline and James Jarvis had both trained at the Fosse Memorial. They were obviously fond of each other. They gave every sign, so Marigold, Hester's middle sister said, of being in love.

But not only Marigold, their parents also thought so. Hester remembered hearing them talking as they inspected the marquee that afternoon before the party, Mother saying,

'Wouldn't it be marvellous if they asked us to announce it tonight?'

But no announcement had come. The gift-wrapped box this man had presented Caroline with had contained a nurse's fob watch instead of a diamond ring. And shortly after the party, just before their parents' accident in fact, he had gone abroad, and had never returned. At least not to Caroline.

Hester's normally gentle eyes sparked with anger. Her cheeks flushed and then paled, as she stared at the man her sister had waited for. This man, tall, handsome and now grown overbearing, who frowned at her own slowness with lofty and unconcealed scorn. As if it were a crime far blacker than betraying a young girl's trust, blacker than ruining a woman's whole life.

Hester's hands shook almost uncontrollably. The green bottle, chilled and bedewed and slippery, slid from her grasp. It crashed to the floor. The glass exploded. The half-released cork popped. The froth of golden liquid cascaded everywhere.

With horror, she heard Mr O'Rourke's gleeful laugh, Sister's indrawn indignant breath and a voice, Mr Jarvis' no doubt, saying sternly, 'Now look what you've done, you clumsy girl.'

As in a nightmare, Hester found herself bending down, forgetful of everything else but to clear the mess and get away. She began scooping up the glass with unthinking despair, till hard, ungentle fingers fastened suddenly round her wrists. She felt herself pulled un-ceremoniously to her feet, and raising her eyes from the white coat, saw Mr Jarvis' stern face,

'Never, but *never*, pick up broken glass in your fingers,' he snapped crossly. 'Don't you know even that? You might easily have . . .' he broke off and clicked his tongue in exasper-ation. 'Too late. You already have cut your-self,' he said accusingly.

Hester flushed in mingled anger, misery and guilt. She kept her eyes fixed on his face. Hopefully, for a second, she thought she saw the faintest softening of concern round his straight mouth, as if momentarily she had been transformed from an inept nurse to a patient. But his deep voice remained sharp with irrita-tion. 'Let that be a lesson to you, Nurse.' And at the same time, he lifted her hand in his own cool capable one, and bent his head to examine the cut on her left index finger. Narrowing his eyes, he pressed his thumb at its base.

It was a strong well-shaped, scrupulously manicured thumb, she remembered thinking with the random remembrance of unimportant detail that comes with shock.

'Can you flex your finger, Nurse?'

Her hand seemed detached from herself. Even the blood which splashed down her white dress, not really hers. But somehow her finger got the message and wiggled obediently.

'Good. You're lucky you didn't sever a tendon. *Then* where would you have been, Nurse?' And in the same breath, without waiting for her answer to his rhetorical question, 'Peter. Come here.'

This was to the most junior of the housemen, Dr Lewis. 'Take her off and put a dressing on it. Check for any fragments. But you should know what to do.' He transferred her hand to young Peter Lewis' warm, eager one.

Oddly enough the transfer made her feel suddenly bereft. She shivered despite the warmth of the day, and Mr O'Rourke, now all concern and penitence, called out dramatically, 'Faith, an' the poor dear girl's going to faint.'

'She can't faint,' Mr Jarvis said crisply and authoritatively. 'She's a nurse.' He turned to Sister, one black eyebrow derisively raised, and added drily, 'Or that is what she is supposed to be.'

His icy tone worked like a dash of cold water in her face.

'I'm perfectly all right, thank you, Mr O'Rourke,' Hester said calmly. She would like to have thanked Mr O'Rourke for his concern. Instead she shot him a grateful smile, before being led towards Sister's office by Dr Lewis.

'Nurses don't come like they used to, I'm

afraid, Mr Jarvis. It isn't only the uniform that
has changed,' Sister said apologetically to the
orthopaedic consultant, and, returning to her
favourite plaint, 'they're too easily got round
these days.'

'Certainly nurses were never so susceptible
in *my* young days, Sister,' Mr Jarvis studied
O'Rourke's case notes which Sister handed
him.

All smiles, Sister answered roguishly, 'I find
that *very* hard to believe.'

'Impossible to believe,' Hester breathed. 'A
lie, in fact.' But only Peter Lewis heard her.

'Don't tell me you've fallen in love with the
Boss,' he asked sympathetically, pushing open
the door, and hooking a stool with his foot so
that he didn't have to let go of her hand. Peter
was a young stockily built man with a shock of
blond hair, and pale blue eyes behind large
horn-rimmed spectacles. The untidy thatch
and the round spectacles made him look
absurdly younger than his twenty-four years.
Deceivingly so, for his eyes were shrewd and
his mouth puggily determined.

'No,' Hester said, her own curving mouth
setting mutinously. 'Quite the opposite.'

'Ah,' Peter sighed, tweezing out a minute
fragment of glass from the cut. 'Heard his
reputation, have you?'

Hester shrugged.

'Well I wouldn't take too much notice if I

were you, even if you had. There's always hospital gossip about a new chap. He's fair game. Especially if he's a bachelor.'

'He's a bachelor still, is he?' For some reason that information both worried Hester and slightly cheered her. Already, her romantic and optimistic nature was beginning to see the distant glimmerings of a possible happy ending. Could James Jarvis' return to the area be connected with Caroline? Was there still hope for their affair? Yet how could Caroline ever be truly happy with such an unfeeling man?

'Ah, yes a bachelor indeed. But why the interest in *that*, if there's no interest to begin with?'

Hester said nothing.

'Come on, Nurse. You arouse my insatiable curiosity.'

Diffidently, Hester answered, 'I know someone who once knew him.'

'A likely story, Nurse!' Peter shook his head. 'There. That's the last of the glass.' He clamped the two lips of the wound together and sighed about the wasted champagne. '*Veuve Cliquot* too, it was. The wedding fizz.' He blinked his eyes sadly. It was rumoured that Peter's mind was very much on weddings. That he had proposed last week to Staff Nurse Leonie Mirfield, but that she had been got round by Mr O'Rourke who had promised to introduce her to the much more glamorous world of show jumping, once he was on his feet again. Staff Nurse Mirfield usually alternated with Sister in charge of the ward. Rarely were both on duty together.

'Like him, did she?' Peter unsealed a sterile dressing. 'This someone who once knew the Boss?'

'How d'you know it was a she?'

'How do I know, Nurse, that you're not going to succumb to your wounds? By intelligence and diagnostic skill. Anyway,' Peter Lewis went on ruefully, 'from what I hear, the Boss leaves a trail of cast-off crutches, mended bones, and broken hearts behind him.' He sighed. His eyes, behind the rounded spectacles became commiserating, 'So don't you be one of them, Nurse Hester. You're too nice a lass.'

'I won't be, I promise. Never. Quite the reverse.'

'Methinks the lady doth protest too much. But I, Nurse Hester, am not feeling exactly over the moon either. The Boss isn't the only one not ten miles from here with a heart of flint stone. Girls in general and staff nurses in particular can be . . .' he shrugged, and broke off with gentlemanly restraint. After a pause, he continued, 'Could we perhaps comfort one another?'

'I've nothing to be comforted about,' Hester

said firmly. 'It's just that I don't like him. Your Boss. I don't trust him.'

'That could be symptomatic of . . .' Peter shook his head sagely, but he didn't specify. His square chunky hands were surprisingly deft. 'There. Does that feel better.'

'Much better, thank you.'

'Good. Glad to be of service.' And then reverting to his previous suggestion, 'Are you off at four?'

'Yes.'

'You live out, don't you? I've seen you cycling in, haven't I? Quite a fetching sight in your blue cape. From a southerly direction.'

Hester smiled. 'From Honeybourne. I live there with my sister.'

Peter brightened. 'I bet you girls get up to some mischief.'

'Far from it. Caroline's the District Nurse. She's much older than I am. Thirty-two. She more or less brought me up.'

Peter blinked questioningly.

'My parents,' Hester said shortly, 'were killed in a car crash.'

'How long ago?' Peter asked gently.

'Ten years. Almost eleven. Caroline had just got her SRN.'

'And were there just the two of you?'

'No. We have a middle sister, Marigold. She's six years older than me. She's the beauty of the family.'

'Married?'

'Yes. Three years ago. They live in Hong Kong.'

Peter said nothing for several seconds. Then he said quietly, 'They tell me there's a good pub at Honeybourne.'

'There is, yes. The Horse and Hounds.'

'Well how about letting me buy you a bar supper. Tonight, if you're free?'

'Not tonight. Caroline and I are going to the cinema.'

'Tomorrow then?'

Hester shook her head. 'I must do some studying.'

Playfully, he touched her little white cardboard cap with its edging of two blue lines. 'Getting ambitious, are you?'

'Not really. Just trying to keep up. I got masses of notes the last time we were in School Block.'

Peter clicked his tongue sympathetically.

Twice a year during their three-year training, the student nurses at the Frantfield and District went back into School Block for clinical lectures. At the end of their period in block they had tests, and random tests at other times when their PTS tutors felt it would be good for them. All this, besides changing wards four or more times a year to make sure they were conversant with as many aspects of nursing as possible.

At the end of each stay on a ward, the student was given a rigorous assessment by the Sister in charge, while during her sojourn on it, her PTS tutor would give her clinical instruction and test her performance on special tasks, such as setting up drips, removing stitches, changing dressings.

Then, after three-year finals, would hopefully come the time to cast off the much disliked white dress, and don the blue cotton and white bib of the SRN and the silver-buckled belt.

'Then how about the day after?'

Hester had time only to nod when the door was pushed wider. Mr Jarvis came striding in. Sister danced attendance, pointing to the telephone. Mr Jarvis had his hand on the bleeper in the top pocket of his white coat. His free hand looked as if to grasp Peter Lewis by the shoulder.

'Surely you've finished a simple dressing like that by now,' he snapped at Dr Lewis. 'Good heavens man, an inch cut not a double amputation.'

'Finished, Mr Jarvis. Yes, sir. We were just going . . .'

'You were just making a date,' Mr Jarvis corrected. 'That is what you were just doing. I heard you. And in duty time.' He picked up the telephone frowning. 'Well, off you go, Dr Lewis. Don't stand there wasting more time.'

His frown deepened as his gaze now included Hester, 'As for you, Nurse. I would have thought you had done quite enough damage for one day.'

CHAPTER TWO

How ironic, Hester thought, mounting her bicycle in the hospital carpark, and free-wheeling down the slope to the lodge, that a man like James Jarvis could ruin her sister's life, and leave a trail of other broken hearts behind him, and yet be so hypocritically indignant about the breaking of a bottle and the making of a very innocuous date.

Waving goodbye to the lodge-keeper, Hester glanced over her shoulder at the rather formidable brick edifice of the hospital behind her. It had been founded in the last century to serve the spa town of Frantfield and its surrounding villages by the famous Dr Fosse who had previously founded the great London teaching hospital that bears his name. Both Caroline and James Jarvis had trained at the Fosse Memorial Hospital which was a pro and an anti for that eminent establishment.

Slowly, Hester pedalled up the slight rise from the hospital to the summit of the first of the three small hills on which Frantfield Wells was built. It was an elegant Regency town, with wide streets, and beautiful though decaying houses, most of them, with a few affluent exceptions, turned into flats or bed-sitters. Each of the three hills was crowned by a church with a tall spire, which gave the town its noted skyline against the back-drop of the Downs beyond.

But Hester's thoughts were not on the sky-line, they were still broodingly on James Jarvis. He was, she decided, altogether too autocratic and unreasonable. Caroline was well out of the whole affair. He would never have treated her kindly, Hester told herself, cycling at some speed past the peeling plaster pillars of Frantfield's pump room, past the white tracery of the bandstand on the Regency Pantiles. He had, after all, deserted Caroline once, and at a time when she most needed him. Marigold and Hester had come to the conclusion that James Jarvis had been unwilling to marry Caroline because she had assumed full and willing responsibility for them both when their parents were killed, giving up her job at the Fosse so to do.

'Caroline will never marry now,' Marigold had said, the night before her own wedding. 'There would only ever be one man for Caroline. Now she's left it too late. She's too set in her ways. Too inward looking. And anyway, these days, her job means everything to her.'

So it did, surely. Though who could really tell with Caroline. She kept her innermost feelings to herself. Even Marigold, six years nearer to her in age than Hester, was never her confidante. Sometimes Caroline treated them more as daughters to be protected, rather than sisters to confide in. Despite this, or perhaps because of it, Caroline had made the last ten years happy and secure for her younger sister: perhaps now, having seen James Jarvis, the time had come when Caroline's younger sister had to protect *her*.

Yet in small modest ways, Caroline was still capable of surprising them. After running their home and doing part-time private nursing Caroline had decided she wanted to be a District Nurse, and a very successful one she had become, throwing herself into the work as if there really was something or someone she wanted to forget. She was held in the highest affection and esteem. Her little purple Mini was a familiar and much looked for sight round the Sussex lanes. Caroline was a press-on, the nurse-must-get-through type. Nothing, not even snow or ice or flood or fog, had ever stopped Caroline.

Coming home like this off early duty, Hester was always prepared to meet the purple Mini speeding somewhere on a call. However, only the sound of tractors, the hum of a harvester in the summer wheatfield underlined the symphony of lark song, blackbirds in the hedge-rows and crickets in the warm grass. Far away to the left, rose the swelling grass flanks of the Downs, the hollows of the chalk quarries glowing softly in the sun.

Now the lane wound its way leisurely between high banks studded with daisies and dandelions. Hester could smell honeysuckle and cut grass and that indefinable sweetness of late afternoon. Bonnington ward, Sister, Mr Jarvis, even Peter Lewis began to fade in the sheer bliss of the bicycle wheels spinning home over the tarmac.

And then, suddenly, there was a honking behind her.

Hester edged closer to the bank, but the honking continued. Glancing over her shoulder, she saw a big and battered green van just fifty yards behind her.

The sharp corner at the withered oak loomed up. She knew it of old—it was quite blind and dangerous.

Hester held up her hand and by shaking her head tried to warn the van driver.

But the honking went on more furiously. The sound of an accelerating engine increased to a roar. Then there was a rush of air from the slipstream as the van overtook the bicycle and skidded out of her view.

Next moment, there was a squeal of brakes, followed by a shrill animal cry of pain, drowned by the sound of an engine accelerating away.

When Hester rounded the corner, the van was a green speck in a cloud of dust. But just ahead of her bicycle wheel in the middle of the road was a little red-brown bundle.

Hester braked hard. The wheels locked solid. Dismounting, she propped the bike against the hedge and slowly walked forward, afraid of what she would find.

The bundle didn't move. But it was alive. Close to she could see a little rust-coloured chest heaving.

She knelt down.

Two green eyes glared at her. They sparked red with terror.

It was a young fox cub, its velvety muzzle curled back from its sharp baby teeth in defiance.

As soothingly as she could, Hester murmured, 'I'm not going to hurt you,' and put out her hand.

Immediately, the cub snapped at the bandaged fingers. Then, panting desperately, it struggled to its feet and tried to limp away. Its right back leg dragged and a dribble of blood began staining the warm macadam of the road. Hester followed behind, but, though obviously in pain, the young fox eluded her.

'Please let me catch you,' Hester begged desperately. 'Don't run away. You'll die if you do.'

But painfully the fox dragged itself away.

Till suddenly the effort was too much. The cub flopped and lay still panting and bleeding.

But it hadn't given up. As Hester approached again, still trying to make reassuring noises, it gave a little puppy-dog bark, hobbled back on three legs and began struggling towards a gate that gave onto Honeybourne Woods—full of dark moist hollows where no doubt it would curl up and die.

The cub might just have succeeded in dragging itself there had not another vehicle come round the corner from the direction of Frantfield Wells. Hester was dimly aware of a quiet engine, gently cut, of a car door discreetly opened but not shut, of a man's shadow, of a pair of legs in well-pressed grey trousers beside her as she crouched.

She had a momentary vision of him in a smart summer suit and cream silk shirt. She looked up into an almost unrecognisable James Jarvis face.

He was snapping the fastenings of a pair of thick driving gloves, and that done he said simply, 'Stay where you are, keep his attention.' He walked softly along the verge, till he was beyond the little fox. Then a couple of strides forward, a sudden lunge carefully timed, a flurry of brown fur, a squeal of pain and anger, and Mr Jarvis was holding the wriggling animal by the scruff of its neck with one hand, and supporting its injured leg with the other.

Hester had an indelible picture of the surgeon holding high his trophy as triumphantly as a schoolboy. Then Mr Jarvis was advancing towards her.

'Nurse,' he said in a tone more irritated than triumphant, 'I can see you haven't quite finished your adventures for the day.'

For a moment Hester swallowed and said nothing except a vague gulp of thanks.

'Now we've got it—what d'you want me to do with the little brute?'

'I . . . I—' Hester floundered.

'It's in pain. Shocked too. Should we put it out of its misery?'

'No . . . oh *no*!' She paused. 'It's not going to die, is it?'

'I'm not a vet, but I'd say it probably would. And in pain.'

He peered down at the struggling animal's leg, rather as earlier on he had examined the cut on her finger. 'What were you going to do with it? Always supposing you could have caught the little devil?'

'Taken it home,' Hester answered promptly.

'Really,' he eyed her cynically. 'Fed it from a bottle, eh? I doubt it's weaned.'

'Yes.' She flushed at his tone. But her mouth shut firmly, her golden brown eyes glittered with determination.

'And where's home, Nurse?'

'Just down there,' she waved at the village nestling on the flank of the Downs. 'Honeybourne.'

'You live out with your parents, do you?'

'I live out with my sister,' Hester said very clearly, as if enunciating a foreign language. 'She's a District Nurse.'

'Of course.' A strange procession of emotions crossed the surgeon's face. Sudden enlightenment, something like sympathy, something like regret, something remotely resembling guilt, then all carefully shuttered away as a kind of emotional visor clamped down. 'It had been bothering me, slightly,' he said smoothly enough. 'I couldn't quite place you. I rarely forget a face. Something in yours reminded me. I remember your sister. Vaguely, that is.'

Hester closed her eyes lest he see the fury in them. So he remembered Caroline, did he? *Vaguely*. He had only ruined all chance of her finding happiness in marriage, that was all. And he remembered her *vaguely*.

She opened her eyes again when Jarvis said, 'What's the matter, Nurse? Not thinking you're going to faint again, are you?' He lifted a gloved hand stained with the fox's blood as if this sight might be the cause of her distress.

She shook her head vehemently. Then, enunciating clearly again, she said, 'I expect my sister remembers *you*, Mr Jarvis. *Vaguely*.'

He shot her a keen look but answered equably enough, 'I hope she does.' And then changing the dangerous subject quickly, 'And will she . . . your sister, or her husband, maybe, allow you to bring in *this*?' He held the cub closer to her nose.

'Caroline isn't married.'

There was, it seemed, a long pregnant pause.

'You surprise me,' Mr Jarvis said politely.

'It surprises *me*,' Hester said. 'Or it used to. But not now. It surprises other people as well.'

Mr Jarvis looked blank and rather bored. 'She was,' he said with polite indifference, 'I seem to remember, an attractive girl.'

'She still is. Very.'

'Good. And the fox cub?' He almost shook it in front of her to return her to the subject on hand. 'Will she object?' I'm not interested in your sister's attractiveness, the gesture said, only will she literally take this blood-stained bundle out of my hands.

'She will welcome it with open arms.' Hester crossed her fingers. Caroline was fond of horses and dogs. But foxes, she was not sure. Many country dwellers had a love-hate relationship with the fox.

'Then I suggest we put your bike in the back, and you let me drive you there.'

'But won't it make an awful mess of your car?'

For the first time Hester turned her attention to Mr Jarvis' car. It was a low slung white Scimitar, and from what she could glimpse of the interior that too was white.

'What other way of getting there do you propose? Putting the animal in your saddle bag? Or wheeling your bike and trying to hold him with one hand?'

'I can leave my bike here. In the hedge. Country people are honest. I'll carry him home and come back for my bike later.'

'Rubbish! Get in.'

For a moment, Hester considered defiance. But Mr Jarvis didn't look like brooking any defiance. Besides, already a fragile tender hope had begun to take root. Perhaps James Jarvis had returned to his old haunts, not just because he had been offered the consultancy at an age when most surgeons would consider themselves lucky to be Senior Surgical Officers, but because he still had some feeling for Caroline. Perhaps he had seen the mistake he had made in leaving her. They were still both unmarried. And why was he driving so near Honeybourne anyway?

She asked him that question, though only with casual politeness, when he had got her to sit in the passenger seat, and to take hold of the cub exactly as he instructed.

'Were you making for somewhere in the area?' she asked as he started up the softly purring engine. 'I don't want to hold you up if you have an appointment, Mr Jarvis.' She blinked her long-lashed eyes innocently.

'I *have* an appointment,' he nodded. 'But that needn't worry you. I thought I'd avoid the main road. My appointment isn't till seven-thirty. I'm dining near Brighton. With an old friend.'

Old friend in his language meant old flame, Hester thought, that was certain. She felt a twinge of disappointment.

'You'll have to keep a firm grip on that brute's neck,' Mr Jarvis advised, 'otherwise it might twist round and nip you. We don't want to patch you up yet again.'

'I hope he didn't nip *you*, Mr Jarvis?'

'She,' Mr Jarvis corrected with a strange grim smile. 'She's a vixen.'

'Oh.'

'And *no*, she did *not*.' He shot Hester a strange derisive look, as if even a wild vixen at bay wouldn't dare to bite James Jarvis. 'I'm too wily a bird to get caught like that.'

Hester tightened her lips but said nothing. Too wily a bird to get caught indeed he was, as Caroline and many an old flame had no doubt found to her cost.

'So,' he began and then broke off and asked, 'What's your first name, by the way?'

'Hester.'

'So how long have you lived here, Hester?'

'Ever since I can remember. First with our parents. Then with Caroline and Marigold.'

'Yes, I remember.' He nodded. 'Your parents . . .' There was a long silence. 'Caroline had just qualified, hadn't she?'

'Yes. She was twenty-one. You came to her party about six months before.'

'I seem to recall a skinny child with a turned-up nose. You?'

'Yes, me. I only saw you the once. Just before the party.'

'And that once you were galloping around on a pony twice too big.' He smiled. Then he turned and scrutinised her. 'You're not like Caroline, are you? She was tall and dark and vivacious as I remember. While you're . . .'

He seemed unable to find the right description for her. His silence suggested nondescript.

'And the cottage is on the left past the church. Am I right?'

'Yes.'

He drove the car carefully over the hump-backed bridge that spanned the stream, past the village school, past the Horse and Hounds with the patch of green lawn and white wrought-iron tables under Cinzano umbrellas, past the garage and the bakery, till he drew up slowly outside the cottage's oak gates.

'Charming,' he said politely, staring out at the white-washed, thatched cottage with the diamond-paned windows. 'I remember it now. The roses have grown taller, the honeysuckle thicker. It's a dream cottage in a dream garden. What more could one ask?'

'A husband,' Hester said, but not aloud.

Then the cottage door opened. Framed in the doorway, stood Caroline, still in her dark blue uniform dress. At first she took in only the white car drawn up outside the gate, and the tall man with his back now to the cottage, carefully helping Hester out of the passenger seat. She came to the conclusion there had been an accident, and came hurrying down the path.

In that way it all seemed to happen for the best. Surprise and anxiety wiped from her face the carefully controlled mask it had assumed over the last few years.

Beneath her severely cut fringe of hair, Caroline's dark brown eyes looked tender and concerned, her rather austere mouth tremulous and vulnerable again.

Then James Jarvis turned. Like that, before Caroline had time to assume that mask again, Hester saw her sister look speechlessly from James Jarvis' face to her own and then back to James Jarvis again.

Her hand flew to her mouth in an oddly

girlish gesture. 'Oh, no,' she whispered. 'No! I can't believe it. No.'

For a moment everyone seemed unable to move or speak, like figures in a dream. But in that pregnant moment, much was clear to Hester. Caroline was delighted to see him. She still obviously cared.

Then Caroline became aware of the fox cub Mr Jarvis had taken from Hester and was holding fastidiously away from him. Glad of the diversion and in almost effusive relief, Caroline welcomed it with the open arms Hester had promised.

'Trust Hester,' she smiled, when Mr Jarvis had finished his account of the finding of the cub. 'She has a penchant for every lame dog.' She patted Hester's shoulder and said, 'Of course she was right to have brought it home. We'll look after the poor thing. It was kind of you to give Hester a lift. To help her, James.' Her smile had now become cooler and warier and more formal. But there was no anger behind the smile, no resentment, and surprisingly, there was no apology in his.

'I was glad to,' he said, smiling. 'Glad that I happened along at the right moment.'

'Well, let's take the poor thing inside.' Almost as a refuge, Caroline seemed to slip into her rôle of bustling nurse. Briskly, she led the way into the cottage. 'I think the kitchen would be the best place, James.'

He smiled. 'Don't ask me to operate on the good old-fashioned, well-scrubbed kitchen table.'

'I won't, I promise.' Caroline smiled. She opened up her surgical bag. 'I didn't realise you were coming to the Frantfield,' she murmured, chattering brightly to him over her shoulder, as Mr Jarvis carefully put the cub where she indicated on the kitchen table and held it firmly.

'Nor did I. My predecessor's coronary was rather more serious than was thought. I was appointed quite quickly.'

Caroline didn't ask him if he had intended getting in touch with her. Instead she turned to her sister.

'Hester,' Caroline jerked her head towards the phone, 'can you look up the number for the vet? I think the one at Radstock is the nearest. He's got a tiny animal hospital, I understand. Ask if he'll come out as soon as possible, will you?'

Then she went over and stood beside Mr Jarvis, so close that their arms brushed. Caroline looked up suddenly at James, and he shot her a curious wry and rather sweet smile. He said something about it being like old times. Then he told her, 'Hold the little beast like that, Caroline, while I take another look. Mmm,' he pointed out something to Caroline and she leaned nearer. Their two profiles,

cameoed against the kitchen window, looked
so well matched and so right.

To allow them a few minutes alone together,
Hester took a long time finding the vet's number. She hesitated for a while between a vet
from just north of Brighton and the man from
Radstock called A. Matherson. She finally
settled on the latter. While she dialled the
Radstock number, she heard Caroline's and
Mr Jarvis' voices from the kitchen as they softly
talked to one another.

A. Matherson answered the telephone in
person. He had a slow voice with just the
slightest Scottish lilt. He would be along as
soon as he had finished surgery. Meanwhile
they were to keep the vixen as quiet as
possible.

Returning to the kitchen, Hester searched
their faces. Surely, she thought, a moment of
something more than concern for the animal,
something more like tenderness of love revived
for one another, passed between them?

If it did, Mr Jarvis deliberately shattered it.
'I doubt she'll live,' he shrugged, frowning.
'But at least you can keep it warm and make it
comfortable. The vet will be able to put it out
of its pain.'

He looked at his watch, and said firmly that
he must be on his way. Then, seeing Hester's
stricken face, he patted her arm in an avuncu-
lar manner as he passed her, 'Don't fret your-

self too much, my dear child, over things you can't do anything about.'

He didn't somehow seem to be talking about the half-dead vixen, for he looked boldly and meaningfully at Caroline as he spoke.

CHAPTER THREE

DESPITE James Jarvis' remarks, a bright and seemingly happy Caroline woke Hester the next morning with the news that the fox cub was still alive and had lapped some milk, in which she'd mixed one of the powders the vet had left.

'Get dressed. Come and see for yourself,' she stood in the doorway of Hester's bedroom, looking as if ten years had rolled away, as if life had suddenly given her another chance, and this time she had discovered she was really in love.

'I think,' Caroline murmured as the two sisters stood side by side in the kitchen surveying the fox, 'that it's the vet who's going to be proved right and not James.' But she spoke Mr Jarvis' name with a special breathless tenderness, and a secret inward-turning smile that told more than words.

'Even your friend James would concede the vet might know more,' Hester remarked drily and saw her sister's colour deepen.

'They were both very kind,' Caroline pronounced with finality, somewhat unfairly, Hester thought, to the vet. For after James

Jarvis' rather condescending help, the vet's had been spontaneous, unhurried and warm-hearted, as if he had been a friend from the past rather than James Jarvis.

The vet had arrived shortly after supper, just as Hester was washing the dishes and Caroline was writing up her notes. He was a big burly man of about forty, with short brown hair, a good-humoured mouth and twinkling hazel eyes. He introduced himself as Alistair Matherson, a Scot by birth and Sussex by adoption. He had declared the cub to be a six-month-old vixen, examined her thoroughly, dressed the leg, and given the prognosis that she had a fighting chance.

He had taken a cup of coffee with them, left some powders for the vixen, and shyly suggested the name of Broddi for her. That was the name, he minded, that the crofters of his native Sutherland used for the fox. It meant 'bush' in Gaelic. His wife had once had a pet dog of foxy colouring, which she had called by that name.

So, Broddi, it was. And as Hester and Caroline hastily swallowed their breakfast, it was apparent that Broddi was doing reasonably well.

'We have a new addition to our family,' Hester whispered to third-year student Sheila Richardson, as they both hurried up the steps to Bonnington ward two minutes before 'Re-

port' was due to begin. Sheila lived in the
Nurses' Home and was always avid for any
family gossip, or any gossip at all for that
matter.

'Save it for afterwards,' Sheila whispered
back, 'Sister's off duty. The lethal Leonie is on.
I never know which is worse.'

That morning it became clear that Leonie
was going to be worse. She had returned from a
holiday in Italy, beautifully sun-tanned, but
annoyed that she had missed Mr Jarvis' first
appearance. She too had heard of Mr Jarvis'
reputation, and she liked what she'd heard.

'First impressions are so important,' she said
to the small mirror in Sister's office, when
'Report' was over and the early day-shift
nurses were about to take themselves onto the
ward. And laying an admonitory hand on
Hester's arm added sharply, 'I hear you dis-
graced yourself, Nurse Stanton!' She frowned
and sighed, 'Well, all I can say,' she returned to
the mirror, 'don't ever let me catch you being
so clumsy again.' And as an afterthought,
'Finger all right?'

'Perfectly, thank you.'

'Dr Lewis manage to dress it?'

'Very well.'

Leonie continued to gaze at her reflection, as
if at that moment it was the only face that
pleased her. Hardly surprisingly. For though
she was not a conventionally pretty girl, she

was endowed with striking looks which she enhanced with perfect make-up and grooming. And though the narrow gentian blue eyes were calculating, her nose classical but too thin, and her mouth narrow, the fine skin, the ash-blonde hair, and willowy figure more than compensated. Her effect on men was lethal.

'Well, off you go!' She turned to Hester again. 'That's all! Don't dawdle! Mr Jarvis, I understand, is going to do the round. And remember, I won't have any incidents like yesterday, while I'm in charge. First impressions are so important!'

First impressions that morning involved a re-doing of the sluices, a re-polishing of the wheelchairs, a throwing out of flowers, which were nowhere near past their prime, a spartan clearing of locker tops, a search of Mr O'Rourke's locker and bedspace. It also involved more consultations with the mirror, Hester noticed as she was checking the X-ray viewer in Sister's office. As if Leonie Mirfield was intent on presenting herself as a sexually attractive woman rather than Sister material.

If Sheila Richardson was to be believed, and sometimes she was, then half the female staff of the Frantfield were also trying thus to present themselves. At a hastily snatched coffee break, having dismissed the advent of Broddi as unnewsworthy, Sheila went on to say that *her* money would be on Leonie.

'She collects scalps,' Sheila said mournfully, 'like I collect records. But I'd swap her my entire Beatles for one single date with Mr O'Rourke or Dr Lewis. Though I'd never dare to even dance with Mr Jarvis, would you?'

'I wouldn't want to,' Hester replied and drained her cup.

An hour later Hester watched Leonie Mirfield's inscrutable face as she helped the staff nurse check the folders of clinical notes. Was she really going to try to hang Mr Jarvis' proud head on that uniform belt which so accentuated her tiny waist? What happened when heartbreaker met heartbreaker? Ironically, Leonie Mirfield was the female equivalent of Mr Jarvis. She, like him, left a trail of broken hearts. They were birds of a feather who in due course might well decide to flock together. Then what chance would dear sweet uncalculating Caroline, and her newly resurrected love, have against competition like that?

'That's almost it, I think,' Leonie Mirfield checked aloud as she leafed through the folders. 'Sergeant Mounsey's blood count is here, yes. Mr Hepworth's biopsy report, yes. Mr O'Rourke's last X-ray . . . no, damn! Isn't here. Wretched man. Why does he have to have so many? What would Mr Jarvis say if it was missing? Run down and collect it will you, Nurse. Hurry. But of course don't run. I'll give them a buzz to tell them you're on your way.'

As Hester left, Staff Nurse Mirfield found time to give herself one more lingering look in the mirror. Then she called after Hester, 'And don't stay gossiping!'

It was unlikely, Hester thought, that anyone would detain her with idle gossip. Even Sheila Richardson found X-ray too busy a place to glean gossip. And on the rare occasions Hester had been to the X-ray department, it had always been crowded with waiting patients, and radiographers flitting feverishly among their apparatus. It was the length of the walk that would detain her.

The Frantfield and District consisted of the original red-brick hospital built in Victorian times, with an Outpatients added between the two world wars.

The new wing was completed in the seventies and connected to the old by a long glassed-in corridor. Bonnington was on the second floor of the old wing, which meant hurrying down four flights of steps, then across a loading yard through Outpatients to the concrete floored glassed-in corridor which connected the old with the much smarter new.

In this new wing, the floor was of thick green rubber tiles and here were the ten private rooms with their pleasant bleached mahogany doors, and their view of the formal gardens set

round a statue of Dr Fosse, the hospital Victorian founder. A florist's boy was just delivering
a bouquet of dark red roses to the Sister's office
at the far end, when the second of the private
doors opened and an irate white-coated figure
hailed Hester without preamble or recognition, 'There you are, Nurse! *At last!*' he exclaimed testily. 'Come in!'

Blinking in astonishment, Hester saw it was
Mr Jarvis. But the recognition was not mutual
. . . He jerked his head peremptorily for her to
come inside the room. And when bemusedly
she stood there, he lightly but firmly grasped
her arm and propelled her within.

'I've had my hand on the bell for the last two
minutes,' he said severely.

'But, Mr . . .' she moistened her lips and
tried to speak up.

'But *nothing*, Nurse! Be quiet. I've had my
say, now that's that. I know you're busy down
that end. But if Miss Phillimore needs an
examination, *I* need a nurse. That is obvious,
isn't it?'

Hester drew in a long breath preparatory to
putting him right on who she was and which
ward she belonged to, but he gave a forbidding
shake of his head, and said to the occupant of
the flower-flanked bed, 'Now, Miss Phillimore,
let me take a look.' He rubbed his hands
together. 'I hope my hands are not cold.'

For the first time, Hester was able to have a

good look at the patient, as she lay back on the pillows, her reddish mahogany-coloured hair spread out like a rich fan, her pansy-brown theatrically trusting eyes gazing up at Mr Jarvis. Another of his about-to-be-broken hearts, Hester thought, a youthful but quite tough one.

'You won't hurt me, will you, James?' Miss Phillimore asked in a pathetic little-girl voice.

'Now, when have I ever hurt you?' His tone was a nice mixture of authority and indulgence. It contained, like the drops of angostura bitters in a good cocktail, a dash of masculine irritation. It was a mixture Miss Phillimore clearly enjoyed. She purred and pouted.

'Never, James. Never. You've been sweet. But I haven't known you very long. And there's always a first time.' The pansy-brown eyes filled with unshed tears.

'Not with me, Miss Phillimore.'

'Oh please don't call me Miss Phillimore.'

'Very well . . . Clare. Now I'm going to examine you.'

He nodded briefly at Hester and obediently she began folding back the patient's covers. Hester speculated as to what injury or illness the poor girl might be suffering from. All Hester could see was that Miss Phillimore was wearing the most delicious confection of a nightgown, a flurry of see-through lace and frills and satin bows. A softly curvacious figure was ill-concealed by the nightgown. And from it protruded a pair of perfectly shaped legs and ankles. Hester's eyes travelled down to the perfect feet. No, not quite perfect feet. The metatarsal joint of Miss Phillimore's left foot had an enlarged outward displacement, a condition known as *hallux valgus*.

It was on this that Mr Jarvis' long thin fingers gently fastened. They travelled up to her beautiful ankle and back to the offending bump again.

Miss Phillimore shivered as much with pleasure as with apprehension, Hester thought.

But Mr Jarvis seemed to assume it was with apprehension. He spoke across the bed to Hester, 'As you know, Nurse, Miss Phillimore is to undergo surgery tomorrow. She is naturally nervous.' And to the patient, smiling slightly disbelievingly, 'Does it *still* hurt?'

'Not *quite* so much,' she blinked her eyes admiringly, 'You have the healing touch, James.'

'I doubt that. Surgeons aren't usually gifted thus.' Mr Jarvis laughed drily and straightened. He himself drew up the covers over Miss Phillimore. Then he lifted her wrist, and checked her pulse with his watch. The pansy-brown eyes looked dreamily content as if the patient could have lain there happily for ever. Then, satisfied with Miss Phillimore's pulse, Mr Jarvis relinquished her wrist. He bent over her, pulled down the lower lids of her eyes, gravely inspecting ostensibly for anaemia, but really, Hester suspected, drowning in their pansy depths.

'Good, good,' he murmured, and then straightened and smiled. 'There's nothing wrong at all, Clare. You didn't need me. The pain was psychosomatic.'

'What does that mean, James?'

'What I said . . . that you didn't need me. I shall see you tomorrow in theatre.' And to Hester, 'That's all, thank you, Nurse. You can go. Next time, *come at once*!'

Thankfully, Hester closed the door behind her. She was just continuing on her way to X-ray when a third-year student came panting along from Sister's office, rushing towards Miss Phillimore's room. 'Heavens,' she gulped, 'I hear Mr Jarvis has been ringing like fury. Needed a chaperon. But we had a post-op emergency in number eight, while Miss Phillimore moans about her big toe. Is Mr Jarvis still on the rampage? What were you doing here? Did you want something?'

'I don't know!' Hester sighed. 'To all those questions, *I don't know*. But I seem to have stood in for you. I think. I don't know why. I just happened to be there.'

'He wouldn't know the difference!' the third-year student cheered visibly. 'Thanks! Thanks a lot! I'll do the same for you some-

time.' With relief, she fell into step beside
Hester. 'I tell you, he wouldn't know. The
consultants say all nurses look alike. And certainly someone like Mr Jarvis would never look
twice at a student.'

Hurrying, Hester agreed vehemently, 'No.
Never.'

'Miss Phillimore's a real looker though, isn't
she?' the third-year student went on, but
Hester with a wave of her hand was disap-
pearing into X-ray, where she grabbed the
envelope handed to her, and scurried back
down the corridor. She arrived on Bonnington
one full flight of stone steps ahead of Mr Jarvis.

She could see his dark head and broad shoulders rounding the curve of the flight below as
she took the final steps two at a time. Mr Jarvis
was followed by the registrar, a senior houseman and the yellow thatch of Peter Lewis.

Staff Nurse snatched the envelope from her.
'I thought I told you to hurry. I have already
warned . . .' she began, when she heard the
sound of masculine feet and Mr Jarvis' deep
voice.

'They were just behind me,' Hester gulped.
'I'm sorry I . . .'

But now a polite sweet smile had replaced
Staff Nurse's frown.

'Put the X-ray in O'Rourke's folder,' she
said, in an altered tone. 'Then go and see to the
coffee. I expect Mr Jarvis will take coffee

later.' She advanced down the corridor to meet them, her hand outstretched.

Conventional greetings and introductions over, Mr Jarvis murmured that he had been asked to see a patient unexpectedly, the nearest a consultant would ever get to an apology for lateness. Bearing in mind his high-handedness, Hester was surprised he made even that.

Then the white coats were advancing to the ward entrance. Hester found her exit blocked. She stood patiently, waiting and watching, her wide-eyed gaze going from face to face, from Mr Jarvis' frugal smile to Leonie's dazzling one.

There was no doubt, Hester thought, that a number of females within the walls of the Frantfield and District hospital were interested in Mr Jarvis. He had just come from drowning in the pansy depths of Miss Phillimore's eyes to the undoubted interest in Staff Nurse's sharper, brighter ones. No wonder he was high-handed and arrogant. No wonder he had forgotten poor Caroline.

As if aware of her gaze, Mr Jarvis turned his head sideways. Momentarily, his eyes met hers. Their expression was strangely, almost exaggeratedly blank. Then he gave an abstracted nod. 'Good morning, Nurse,' he said coolly, a slight frown drawing together his black brows. 'I've seen you before, haven't I? I seem to remember you.' He took a quick look at her face. 'Vaguely.'

It was one of those outwardly harmless, inwardly traumatic moments. It was as if he was demonstrating how totally anonymous she was to him, that he had utterly forgotten he had seen her only a few moments before. He had forgotten the incident with the vixen. He had forgotten she was Caroline's sister. He had forgotten Caroline. He was totally indifferent. It was at that moment, Hester afterwards told herself, that she really began to hate him.

CHAPTER FOUR

'Oh, I don't think you really hate him,' Peter Lewis said judiciously as they sat under the striped Cinzano umbrellas on the lawn of the Horse and Hounds. The summery weather was holding, and the air was heavy with the scent of honeysuckle and roses and the fragrance of coming autumn. Hester had put on her pink linen pedal pushers with matching top and Peter looked younger than ever in jeans and sneakers. 'I'd like to meet the woman who really did,' he added.

'You've already met one.'

'I don't believe it.'

'Not only met one but put a dressing on her finger. And now you've just bought her a cider.'

Peter clinked his glass with hers. 'The finger seems to be healing. But I see you've replaced my work of art with a common plaster.'

'It's as good as new. And I do hate him.'

Peter shook his head. After a decent pause he asked, 'And how about Leonie? Did she seem taken with him?'

'Not that I noticed,' Hester said firmly. A less kindly girl might certainly have said that

49

Staff Nurse had gone out of her way to please the orthopaedic surgeon, had hung on his every word, had plied him with coffee and compliments, had continued the case conference afterwards until well into lunch time.

'Maybe she still prefers O'Rourke.' Peter drained his glass. 'O'Rourke's rich and reasonably famous. He hobnobs with the gentry. Gets invited by Lord this and the Duke of that.'

'I don't think she prefers anyone,' Hester said, and that at least was utterly true. She kept them all guessing. And she was always careful not to step beyond the bounds of professional propriety.

Staff Nurse had seemingly been well pleased with Mr Jarvis' visit, and having been brusque with Mr O'Rourke earlier on, had gone out of her way to be sweet and charming. She had shown interest in the point-to-point he was watching on television, and asked him flatteringly for his explanation of the finer points of the meeting.

'She certainly doesn't prefer *me*,' Peter Lewis was still turning over Hester's last remark.

Hester smiled comfortingly. 'Well, you're not as persistent as Mr O'Rourke.'

'Nor as attractive as the Boss.'

'He isn't attractive,' Hester began vehemently, and then meeting Peter's amused gaze finished, 'well, only in a certain way.'

'That certain way seems to get the girls going.'

'*Some* girls.'

Peter laughed and caught her hand. 'Tell me really why you don't like him.'

'He's so ruthless.'

'An orthopod has to be.'

Hester shrugged.

'You see, you've only seen him on the ward. Maybe off duty . . .'

'I've seen him off duty.' Hester found herself embarking on the story of Broddi.

Peter heard it through, then said judiciously, 'The Boss seems to have behaved very reasonably. He gave you his valuable time and his opinion . . . his professional opinion, free,' adding 'I mean, lots of people wouldn't have stopped and helped you.'

'He couldn't have got past. Not unless he'd run right over the pair of us.'

'But he took the pair of you home.'

'I said he was ruthless, not a monster. And anyway, when he got us home, he couldn't wait to get away again. He didn't like poor Broddi dripping blood over his white upholstery.'

'Who would?' Peter murmured.

'He didn't,' Hester finished, 'really do anything for the poor thing.'

'Well, that was the vet's job. You said you rang for him.'

'Yes, I did. And that was just the difference.

He didn't know us but he came straight away,
Well, almost. And he was so sweet and gentle
and humane. He had a real way with animals.'

'That's what vets are supposed to have, they
tell me.' Peter smiled. 'Sounds as if he had a
real way with humans too.'

'Yes, he had. He made us feel much better.
Much more confident. He even gave us the
name of Broddi for her. He was all fatherly
and cuddly in an old tweed jacket and cor-
duroys and riding boots, if you know what I
mean?'

'Oh, very clearly,' Peter's smile became wry.
'Not all white coat and stethoscope?'

'No. And he thinks Broddi has a fighting
chance. He set the leg and gave her a pain
killer. She slept all night. And he told us how
to make up dried milk so that it's not too
rich. While all Mr Jarvis said was it would
probably die. And should he put it out of its
misery.'

Peter shrugged. After a moment, he said, 'I
hope you didn't confound him with that diagnosis this morning.'

Hester shook her head. 'He never once
asked about the fox. He'd forgotten about
her.'

'He'd have other things on his mind,' Peter
said loyally.

'He'd forgotten the whole incident. He
didn't even remember *me*,' Hester was

alarmed to hear a note of indignation creep into her voice at that last sentence.

'Shame,' Peter said, hearing it too. Then regretfully, 'Perhaps he was too absorbed in Leonie.'

'No. It wasn't that. I'd seen him before. By myself. Before he met Leonie. He didn't recognise me then. Not at all. He thought I was a nurse on the private wing.'

'Nurses all look alike to me,' Peter said, 'unless they're . . .'

'Called Leonie,' Hester teased.

Peter blushed. 'Sorry. I'm being tiresome, aren't I. But you know what I mean. Unless there's something distinctive like being a staff nurse or sister. They're meant to. A nurse is a nurse is a nurse. Except for you, of course,' he went on, trying to be kind but floundering. 'You've got such a nice face.'

'Nice,' Hester echoed doubtfully.

'You've also got beautiful eyes,' Peter said, holding up his glass to them, 'and I don't want you to get the wrong idea of what I feel about Leonie. It isn't as the grapevine has it. She doesn't really compare to you.' He seemed about to embark on some explanation. But the landlord's wife picked that moment to bring out a tray laden with her plates of home-cured ham and salad with new potatoes from the garden, minted and buttered, and wedges of Bramley apple pie and Jersey cream to follow.

When it was cleared away, the time for explanations and his absorption with Leonie seemed to have gone. Peter sighed contentedly.

Darkness had fallen. Fairy lights had been lit in the horse-chestnuts surrounding the lawn. They glowed green and red on the spiky balls of the conker nuts. A romantic sickle of moon hung above the tree tops.

When Hester looked at her watch and said it was high time she was getting home for her sister was out and Broddi would be needing another bottle, nothing would satisfy Peter but that he should come too.

'After all, I'd like to see the little vixen. Why shouldn't she now have the benefit of the incomparable Peter diagnosis?'

'With apologies to the Boss,' Peter said an hour later, 'my diagnosis comes down on the side of the vet. That cub's going to live. And be a damned nuisance to everyone.'

'I'm delighted to hear it,' Hester smiled. They were standing in the cottage's cheerful kitchen while Hester made coffee on the Aga for themselves and made up a bottle for the vixen. The cub, Peter's brief inspection of it over, was now again curled in a basket on the hearth. Her green eyes looked up at Hester expectantly.

'Greedy little devil, isn't she?' Peter said a

few minutes later, watching Hester gently tuck it under one arm and, sitting herself on a high pine stool, give it the bottle with the other. 'Sucks like a piglet. How soon before it stops being on the bottle and starts on the neighbours' chickens?'

Hester shuddered. 'I don't know. We'll have to give it a little raw meat pretty soon. But foxes eat insects and vegetables too. They particularly like wasps' nests, Alistair Matherson said.'

'Alistair Matherson? He's the fatherly vet in the tweed jacket, is he?'

'Yes.'

'Met him before, had you?'

'No. We haven't any animals. So we've never had to call a vet. And Alistair . . . Mr Matherson lives about six miles the other side of Honeybourne.'

'With his wife?'

'I presume so. Why?'

Peter shrugged. 'No particular reason. Just that you seem to like him.'

'I like lots of people.'

'Lots of men?'

'Not necessarily men. Besides, I don't know lots of men. Except in the ward. I like *them*. All of them.'

'You know *me*.'

'Yes. And I like you.'

'I'm not sure I'm pleased to be herded

together with the patients,' Peter began, when the telephone rang.

'Oh, heavens,' Hester exclaimed, 'I can't put her down. Will you answer it, Peter. Tell whoever it is that Caroline's *off* duty. She's gone to Brighton. If it's an emergency there's a number they can ring on a message pad, just on the left of the phone.'

Peter walked through into the pretty oak-beamed and chintzy sitting-room. She heard him lift the receiver, and then a curious conversation followed. 'I'm sorry,' Peter Lewis began, like a recording machine, 'the District Nurse is out. If you would care to leave a message, or if it's an emergency, hang on,' she heard him pick up the information card that stood by the phone. 'There is a number here where . . .' He broke off suddenly, 'Who am I, did you say? Who the blazes am I? Me? Yes, as a matter of fact this *is* Lewis, Dr Lewis, Peter Lewis, how did you know? Yes, your voice is familiar too. Oh, it's *you*, sir. *Sorry*. Sorry, sir. Didn't expect *you* to be calling *here*, as it were. Sorry, sir. As I say, the Nurse is out! What the hell am I doing here? Well, sir . . . yes, Hester, Nurse Stanton is here, of course. Why isn't she answering the phone? She's . . . she's busy. Feeding the . . . Well, sir, if you insist, yes you do, of course . . .'

There came the sound of the receiver being laid down carefully, Peter put his head round the kitchen door. 'Hester, put that damned cub down! Come to the phone! Quick about it! The Boss wants a word with you!'

CHAPTER FIVE

'SO WHY exactly did James Jarvis phone?' Caroline asked Hester, as she poured the breakfast coffee the next morning.

They were sitting on the little brick patio at the back of the cottage, enjoying the unusually warm September weather. Broddi, the fox cub, lay in her basket on the doorstep, blinking her eyes and watching the Red Admiral butterflies on the Michaelmas daisies with anticipatory relish. Hester sighed. Alistair had warned them that foxes ate butterflies. But it was not of their fate that Hester was thinking. She was thinking of other predators. James Jarvis in particular, and the question Caroline had just asked was one she had asked herself most of the night. Why would he have phoned if he wasn't interested in renewing his affair with Caroline?

'To speak to you,' Hester answered at last, sipping her coffee.

'You're sure?'

'Yes. He asked for *you*.'

'Did he say he'd phone again?'

'Not precisely. But I got the impression he would.'

She took a quick surreptitious glance at Caroline's face to see how she was taking this information. Her sister's normally healthy colour had deepened, a faint tender smile played around her lips.

'I should think he'll phone some time today,' Hester drained her cup.

'I shall be home at lunchtime. Alistair said he'd look in and dress Broddi's leg. But I'll be out after that on visits. And this evening, I have the committee meeting for the Red Cross Fête.'

She is both hopeful and afraid, Hester thought, feeling suddenly the older and wiser of the two of them. She is afraid to commit her feelings to him again. Perhaps it is all too late. Perhaps she is afraid to return his tentative advances. Even if love knocked on the door Caroline might well now be afraid to open it.

'You should give yourself more time off,' Hester said gently, 'more relaxation. You work too hard.'

'I enjoy it,' and in the same breath as if she had been pondering Mr Jarvis all this time, 'I suppose James didn't leave any message?'

'No.'

'Then it can't have been very important, can it?' Caroline sounded disappointed. She looked at her watch as if she'd wasted too much time on a red herring. 'I expect he just phoned to ask about Broddi.'

'That was the excuse he made.'

'Why didn't you say so before?' The disappointment deepened.

She's interested in him still, Hester thought, but she's afraid to make the slightest move for fear of a rebuff.

'Because, as I say, it was the *excuse*. Not the reason. The real reason was that he wanted to talk to you. I could tell.'

'How?'

'I just could.'

'And why would he want to speak to me?'

'Because you're an old friend.'

Caroline nodded but looked not quite convinced.

'And he's lonely.'

'Lonely?' Caroline's beautiful eyes widened in astonishment. 'Lonely, did you say Hester? James Jarvis *lonely*!'

Hester nodded her head, hoping against hope that she was doing and saying the right thing.

Caroline stared at her thoughtfully for several seconds, 'Nonsense, he's never lonely. He's only got to crook his little finger and half any hospital comes running,' Caroline's voice took on an unaccustomed asperity.

'You sound just like Peter Lewis.'

'Peter Lewis? Oh, yes! *Dr* Lewis! The young man you were entertaining last night.' Caroline raised her brows.

'Now you sound like Mr Jarvis himself.'

'I seem to be becoming quite an impersonator.' Caroline stood up, 'And how did *he* sound?'

'*Very* disapproving. Very strait-laced. Poor Peter was quite dashed. I'm not sure what he said to him. Mr Jarvis had the nerve to ask *me* if my sister knew I was entertaining men at *that* time of night.'

Caroline said lightly, 'And well he might. What did you say?'

'I said I *thought* so.'

'And?'

'And he replied, I surprised him. Then he went on to lecture me. Mostly about student nurses needing their rest.'

'Well, you know these consultants,' Caroline slipped her hand in her pocket and brought out her appointments book. 'Their idea of student nurses.'

'He sounded less like a consultant,' Hester said boldly, watching Caroline's face, 'more like an irate elder brother.'

Momentarily Caroline's expression froze. Then she recovered and said lightly, 'Yes, that sounds like the James Jarvis I know.'

And love? Hester wondered. That was how the phrase ended wasn't it? And wasn't that what Caroline meant? Wasn't she giving all the signs of still being in love with Mr Jarvis but, as before, being too shy, too sweet, too nice to pin him down. Leaving the field clear for the Miss Phillimores and the Leonie Mirfields.

Emboldened by that theory Hester went on to try to give her sister one last push in the right direction. 'But despite his disapproval of me . . .'

'Not *of you*,' her sister looked up from her appointments book to correct mildly, 'of your entertaining Dr Lewis in the early hours.'

Hester shrugged, 'Well, despite whatever he disapproved of I still got the impression he was lonely. I mean even an attractive man can get lonely can't he? Lonely for companionship?'

'Yes,' Caroline agreed in a voice torn by indecision.

'I felt,' Hester went on, her imagination warming to her subject, 'that he was angling for an invitation.'

Caroline snapped the appointments book shut with a certain finality. Her brown eyes, a shade darker than her sister's but yet so like them in their clarity and candour, stared searchingly into Hester's face.

What she saw there did not seem to reassure her. She looked unhappy and vulnerable, as if the thought of James needing her again, even for companionship, set up a warring whirlpool of unhappy memories and happy possibilities.

'You know,' she said softly, 'that I was quite friendly with James Jarvis a long time ago. When Mother and Father were alive?'

The question was rhetorical. Hester nodded and waited expectantly.

'There's a lot though about my friendship with him that you *don't* know. Few people did. And it all happened before you were old enough to understand.'

Hester said nothing. Much older sisters, even perceptive ones like Caroline, rarely realised how much a child saw and understood. Besides, what she hadn't seen, Marigold had told her.

'James is . . .' Caroline tried to continue and then broke off. She gave a despairing little shrug at the impossibility of explaining James and how she felt about him.

'I think I understand,' Hester said softly. 'More than you think.'

Her sister looked at her gratefully. 'Then you understand he's not the sort of man to be *pursued*.'

'Asking him to tea, or to the Red Cross fête, or for a drink, or just being friendly could hardly be said to be *pursuit*,' Hester protested.

'It could be said to be trespassing on a previous friendship,' Caroline said primly.

It was Hester's turn to exclaim, 'Nonsense! Besides, you want to, don't you?'

'Of course I do.'

'You still like him, don't you?'

'Of course.'

'Well, then?'

'Well, then,' Caroline gently mimicked her. Pointedly she looked at her watch, 'It's time we were both on our way. One of these days you'll understand why *I* don't want to be the one to do the inviting, why James has to come out of his corner and make *his* position clear.'

Hester thrust out her full lower lip the way she did when she was frustrated. Her eyes filled with tears of disappointment. How, she wondered, could Caroline be so blind and so conventional? How could she and Mr Jarvis let their chance of happiness slip away from them yet again, while they waited for the other to make their position known?

'You don't understand, do you?' Caroline said gently, patting her sister's head as she walked briskly back into the kitchen. She shooed Broddi into her usual corner, and added, 'Never mind, Hester. One day, when you really know what love is you, then you might begin to.'

'Resist beginnings, all too late the cure, an' I'm quoting from the saintly Thomas Aquinas, in case you didn't know,' Mick O'Rourke said to Hester, as she tried to push him in the wheelchair towards the ablutions. 'I'll push myself. Then I don't get into lazy habits. Mr Jarvis likes his patients to be independent. Now isn't that a fact?'

'It is indeed,' Hester nodded.

She had seen nothing of Mr Jarvis for the best part of a week. Wednesday he had been operating. Thursday, the registrar had done the round. Friday he had done it himself but Hester had been in the sluices, re-cleaning the bedpans to Sister's satisfaction and had not seen him. Saturday he had made a brief appearance to look at old Sergeant Mounsey, a hip replacement patient from the British Legion home. Staff Nurse had accompanied him.

Hester mentally logged all these missed encounters with Mr Jarvis because she had already made up her mind that if anything was to be done about these star-crossed lovers, it would have to be done by her. For during all that time of not seeing James Jarvis, Caroline had made it quite clear that she did not want to discuss him again with her sister, that she was far too immersed in her patients and in village affairs like the fête to give James Jarvis a second thought.

The Red Cross fête was indeed the staple subject of conversation next, of course, to Broddi, at Honeybourne cottage, and it was of the fête that Hester chatted to Mr O'Rourke as she walked beside his self-propelled chair out into the corridor. A fortune-teller from the sea-front at Brighton had offered her services free, the donkey man from Eastbourne was bringing his string. The Rector's wife and the

GP's wife were making cream teas. Caroline was doing the jumble, and Hester the tombola and the raffles.

'Sure an' I'll tell all my horsey friends to go,' Mr O'Rourke said. 'They're the big spenders. And bring me some raffle tickets. I'll make the lads in here buy the lot. An' I'll give you a prize for your tombola, Nurse. It'll be the best prize on the stall. 'Tis the least I can do.'

'So long as it isn't a bottle of *Veuve Cliquot*,' Peter Lewis came bounding up the steps into the ward corridor and immediately joined in the conversation. Out of the corner of his mouth, he said, 'The Boss is just one hundred yards behind me and closing in fast. And he's not in the best of moods, so no dropping of bottles or bricks, please Mr O'Rourke or Nurse Hester.'

That Mr Jarvis was not in the best of moods immediately became clear. Hester had just helped Mr O'Rourke to the washbasin, when she came face to face with the surgeon.

A flicker of irritation drew together his dark brows. His eyes narrowed as if trying momentarily to place her. 'Find Sister,' he told Hester peremptorily. 'Don't stand there doing nothing. I'm in a hurry.'

'Back in a moment,' she called to Mr O'Rourke and then fled down the ward to the balcony where Sister and the social worker were trying to explain to Mr Cuckney that he would need to have a home help when he was discharged, no matter how much he hated to have a woman round his kitchen.

Hester was immediately then sent off to return Mr O'Rourke to his bed, to summon the OTs and the Physios, and to see to the coffee for the case conference afterwards.

The conference broke up an hour and a half later. Mr Jarvis stalked off down the corridor with Sister in attendance, without giving anyone else a second glance.

'The Boss had two emergency ops early on. Crack of dawn,' Peter Lewis explained, coming into the ward kitchen where Hester was washing up, to scrounge anything that was edible. 'Motorcycle accident. He's half dead on his feet.'

'We didn't get them up here.'

'No. They're in IC. The Boss has just gone off to talk to the relatives.'

'Are the cyclists all right?' Hester dried her hands, buttered a piece of bread and handed it to Dr Lewis.

'They will be. No thanks to them. Doing seventy on a country road.' He wolfed down the bread and then regarded the rest of the loaf greedily.

'Is that your lunch?' Hester asked him severely, pulling out more slices from the wrapper.

'And breakfast.'

Hester sighed. 'You should eat properly. Can't you go down to the canteen?'

'Not a hope. The Boss wants to see a woman in Chichester next. It's all go, go. Well, thanks for the food. Best not be caught in here. Sister would skin me.'

In the event, it was not Sister who caught him, but, by a whisker, Mr Jarvis himself. Peter Lewis had just hurried into the corridor as Mr Jarvis returned. Through the half-open door through which Peter had made his exit, Hester could clearly be seen at the sink. Peter Lewis was wiping off the bread and butter from his lips and his guilty expression obviously did not go unnoticed.

Mr Jarvis thrust his hands into the pockets of his white coat and looked from one to the other. His expression was thunderous. 'Entertaining yet again, are you, Nurse?' he asked acidly, before sweeping Peter along with him to Chichester, the women's orthopaedic ward.

Clearly Mr Jarvis' antipathy to herself made her rôle of self-appointed cupid an impossible one.

To make matters worse, the other half of the matching pair proved just as elusive. Babies being born in the environs of Honeybourne seemed to assume epidemic proportions. And Caroline was here there and everywhere except at Honeybourne cottage, so that Hester never had an opportunity to try to bring James Jarvis and her sister together.

Sister Bonnington proved no cupid either. Hester always seemed to be going on duty as Caroline was coming off and vice versa. 'Well we both work unsocial hours,' Caroline said equably when Hester remarked that they saw even less of each other these days, as they literally passed on the garden path, Caroline to dress old Mrs Paisley's ulcerated leg, and Mr Johnson's orbital collulitis, Hester to rush into the cottage for a bath and go to bed.

'Unsocial and unromantic,' Hester said, though not aloud.

In the end, it was Mr O'Rourke who consciously or unconsciously played cupid. Five days later, on Mr Jarvis' next round, the Irishman produced from his locker some books of Hester's raffle tickets, which he'd been flogging with great success round the ward.

Sister frowned furiously and shook her head, and when these silent warnings were ignored said, 'Don't let Mr O'Rourke get at you, Mr Jarvis.'

But Mr Jarvis was in an approachable mood. The two motorcyclists were now out of danger and had come from Intensive Care to the ward, where they were improving rapidly and to whom Mr Jarvis had just delivered himself of a stern lecture on the error of their cycling ways. Sergeant Mounsey's laminectomy was doing better, and there was about the ward a feeling of getting well.

'It's all in a good cause, Sister,' Mr Jarvis flicked his white coat back and dived into his trouser pocket for the money. 'I'll have a couple of books.'

His housemen and the physios and the OTs and the social worker followed suit.

'We've all bought tickets in here, sir,' Mr O'Rourke was unusually well-behaved and ingratiating that morning. 'Every man-jack. So there should be a winner amongst us to celebrate.'

Shades of Mr O'Rourke's fictitious birthday celebrations and the broken bottle of *Veuve Cliquot* must have crossed Mr Jarvis' mind for he raised one eyebrow and smiled ironically. 'Not *too* great a celebration, I hope, Mr O'Rourke.'

'Oh, no, sir! Bless you no! But in hospital, you have to make a lot of a little, if you know what I'm after meaning.' His Irish eyes looked mournful. 'It all helps to relieve the monotony, begging the nurses' pardon for they try to relieve it, bless 'em. An' we can't go in person. More's the pity. Do I take it *you* will be going, sir?'

Mr Jarvis looked surprised. 'I hadn't thought about it.'

'Oh, but you should, Mr Jarvis. Indeed you should. If only to see we all get fair play on our tickets, sir. See if the Sergeant over there gets the record player he's set his heart on. An' like you say, sir, it's all in a good cause.'

'Well, I'll see what I can do.' Mr Jarvis handed back Mr O'Rourke's case folder to Sister and prepared to move on. His mood was still human and approachable, but he eyed Mr O'Rourke shrewdly, as if he suspected he had more than Red Cross raffle tickets up his sleeve. 'It might prove to be quite entertaining.'

'Thank you, sir.' Mr O'Rourke waved his ticket stubs as if winning the raffle was as important to him as winning the Oaks.

Why then, Hester wondered, as she followed the team out, did the Irishman give her that strange knowing wink and put up his thumb?

CHAPTER SIX

'But that's my very best dress,' Caroline protested that night before the Red Cross fête, when supper cleared away, and Broddi settled down after her last feed, they were discussing what they would wear. 'I can't possibly wear such a good dress to serve on the jumble stall.' She favoured Hester with a suspicious not unkind look, rather like the one Jarvis had favoured O'Rourke with, as he endeavoured to get him roped in for this self-same event. 'What's on your mind, Hester?'

'Nothing. Merely that you look so nice in that lettuce green.'

'But that's my wedding-and-christening dress and it's much too grand.'

'Staff Nurse Mirfield is coming and she bought a dress specially. Blue silk. Got it in the sales. And some new sandals.'

'Really?' A spark of amusement lit Caroline's eyes.

'A whole lot of people are coming from the hospital.'

'They usually do, darling.'

'Sister would have come, but she's on duty. She said it was probably a good thing because only *she* can put the fear of God into Mr O'Rourke and he's getting restless now he's on the mend.'

'It's always the way,' Caroline agreed, sorting the jumble that needed to be mended into a pile, and opening her workbox.

'Who else is coming,' Caroline asked, 'that I've heard you talk about?'

'The nice theatre porter, Mr Gainsborough, is coming. And several of the physios and Peter Lewis. And rumour hath it, maybe, Mr Jarvis.'

There, the name was out. Hester watched her sister's face.

'Only maybe?' Caroline asked in a strange tone.

'Only maybe,' Hester repeated.

Caroline looked up. For a moment darker brown eyes stared keenly into golden brown. Hester kept hers studiously innocent.

'You didn't ask Mr Jarvis, did you, I hope?' Caroline asked sharply.

'No, certainly not! I never mentioned the fête to him, let alone *asked* him.'

'Good,' Caroline looked relieved. 'It wouldn't be . . . I wouldn't want . . .' she didn't say what she wouldn't want. She simply flushed and looked embarrassed. And changing the subject back to the safer one of clothes, said, 'Perhaps I'll wear my caramel-coloured cotton.'

'That old one with the white piping?'

'It's not old, darling. Only a couple of years.'

'More like three or four or five.'

'But I've hardly worn it.'

Hester sighed. At least it was better than the even older skirt and top Caroline had been proposing to wear. The colour suited her eyes, but it was a little too sensible.

Just before her sister retired upstairs to have a shower and wash her hair, Hester tried again. 'I was looking through that photograph album on the desk. There's a very nice one of you on holiday in Scotland. I like the way you used to wear your hair.'

Caroline was mending the sleeve in an evening coat that had been given for her stall. She looked up and asked wryly, 'What's wrong with the way I wear it now?'

'Nothing. It's just a little too plain.'

Caroline smiled affectionately.

Hester persisted. 'You used to wear it with a little flick upwards. More bouncy instead of dead straight. It suited you. And that style is coming back into fashion.'

Caroline's smile deepened into outright laughter.

Hester refused to be laughed out of court. She persisted doggedly. 'Let me give you a shampoo. You know I'm quite good at it. I was much in demand on geriatrics. If you don't like the way I set it, I'll wash it out again.'

'Dear Hester,' Caroline said, touching her hand. 'You're very sweet. But also very innocent. Love, darling, isn't a matter of a pretty dress and nicely done hair. It's much much more.'

All the same, she allowed Hester to experiment with setting lotion and scissors and curlers. The result in the morning was, even Caroline admitted it, quite becoming.

Half an hour after Hester had finished combing out her sister's hair and while she was wrestling with her own thick unruly curls, the front door bell rang. Caroline was busy downstairs pricing the last items of jumble. Hester heard her brisk footsteps and the sound of the door being thrown open.

A man's deep voice said, 'Caroline! My dear! How charming you look!'

Hester's heart leapt hopefully for a moment. But the voice was not quite deep enough. Peering over the banisters, she saw the thick-set broad-shouldered figure of Alistair Matherson, the vet, standing in the hall. The sunshine coming in the open door lit his rugged sunburned face. His smile for Caroline was so genuine and so admiring that Hester's heart warmed afresh to him.

'Thought I'd help you along to the fête with all that clobber and take a look at young Broddi at the same time.'

Then he caught sight of Hester coming down

the stairs. His smile widened. He pretended to whistle.

'It's a garden fête, girls. Not a beauty competition,' he shook his brown-haired head. 'Though you'd both win if it were.'

Caroline laughed as gaily as a young girl. 'Oh, why can't surgeons be as relaxed and comforting and warm-hearted as vets,' Hester asked herself. 'If only,' she thought watching the pair of them disappear into the kitchen, 'if only Mr Jarvis will come to the fête and see Caroline like this!'

Mr Jarvis did come. But it seemed doubtful if he would see Caroline at all. He arrived at the Fête-ground, which was in Glebe field just behind the Rectory, with a large party in which the most important person to him was clearly the ex-patient, Clare Phillimore, leaning fragilely on a stick. She was wearing a cream lace dress with a high Edwardian neck threaded through with ribbon, and a wide-brimmed cream straw hat to match. Her parents appeared to be in the party too, and a pale-faced intellectual young man who vaguely resembled them who might have been her brother. Peter Lewis was tagging along with this party, so were a couple of other housemen, as if this were another kind of surgical round. And to complete such an appearance, Staff Nurse Leonie Mirfield was close behind Mr Jarvis, walking gracefully despite very high-heeled shoes and tight elegant silk skirt.

They drove into the fête ground, under the buntinged entrance in three cars, a Rolls, a Rover and Mr Jarvis' white Scimitar. Hester watched them as she turned the wheel of her tombola drum for about the two hundredth time. It was a fine cloudless day and the fête was crowded. Hester wore her coollest frock of yellow cotton with a square neck and narrow shoulder straps, and she could feel the sun burning the bare skin of her arms. Despite the other attractions, the donkey rides and the children's merry-go-round, the bowling for a pig and the Frantfield Foxhounds display of pack control, there had been a constant queue at the tombola for the exciting prizes she had managed to get donated. Mr O'Rourke's case of champagne had already been won by the postmistress, Mrs Judd, to the delight of every-one, for her daughter had just had a baby son delivered by Caroline, so a christening was in the offing. But there were still many excellent prizes—bottles of perfume and toiletries, handbags, bottles of spirits, toys and games waiting to attract the new arrivals.

They were a long time in coming. Then it was Peter Lewis first, extravagantly buying a dozen goes, all of them blank except for the last which won him a skipping rope.

'Too dangerous for me at my age,' he said,

awarding it to the first little girl waiting in the queue. 'I've lost my other hospital pals,' he said to Hester. 'When I saw the beautiful limping Clare she was trying to lure Mr Jarvis into the fortune teller's tent.'

'With any success?' Hester asked.

'Totally without.' Peter smiled. 'He chivalrously helped her to the stall, paid for her ticket, but said he'd go for a stroll while she listened to her nonsense. The last I saw of him he was heading in *this* direction.' Peter suddenly looked at Hester's face with parodied clinical intentness, 'Now why does the mention of seeing the Boss *always* make you look hot and bothered.'

'It doesn't,' Hester denied promptly, dabbing her forehead with her handkerchief. 'It's just that I'm hot. Not bothered. Just baking hot.'

'My dear girl. Of course. How thoughtless of me. Your pitch is full in the sun. I diagnose acute thirst, possible threatened dehydration, and I prescribe iced lemonade. The which I shall immediately go and fetch you from yonder soft drinks stall.'

'Oh, thanks Peter, I'd love some.'

'If I don't return I will have died of thirst myself in that long queue.'

Hester smiled at him gratefully, and resumed the turning of the tombola drum. She had served another three adults and two children, when she saw Mr Jarvis join the queue. He was looking very handsome in white linen trousers and a navy blue open-necked shirt. His arms and neck were brown, and he looked relaxed and young and happy. Just as Caroline did today. How right they were for each other she thought with a strange little twist inside herself, half of pleasure, half of pain.

'Business seems to be good, Hester,' Mr Jarvis said gently when his turn came. She felt so overcome that he should remember her name and say it with such a delightful inflection that she was quite incapable of replying to him. She watched him take out his wallet and hand her a note and it was as well he said, 'Keep the change,' for she found herself unable to calculate it.

She took the note and dropped it in the bowl with the rest of the money, then spun the drum and opened it up for him. She watched his well-shaped hand as he picked up five paper cylinders, 'You can have more if you want, for your pound,' she suggested.

He shook his head bemusedly and seemed to stare at a point above her head.

'You unwrap them, sir,' Hester said, as he appeared to be a novice at the game. 'If there's a number on you get the prize that has the same number.'

But he only glanced at the papers without interest. 'Which stall is your sister serving on,

Hester?' he asked suddenly as if that was the sole reason for coming to the tombola, his sole interest in the fête. 'Where can I find her?'

'She's over there on the far right, just before the swings. On the jumble stall.'

'How singularly inappropriate,' James Jarvis said making an immediate bee-line for the jumble stall.

For a moment, Hester watched his tall form dwindling. Then she heard young Billie Dickinson, who did the paper round and who was the next in the queue, say, 'Look Miss, that gent was in a dream. He's gorn and left 'is wallet.'

Billie put two fingers to his lips and tried to attract Mr Jarvis' attention with a shrill whistle. But Mr Jarvis was either out of earshot, or too absorbed in finding Caroline.

It was a sure sign he was in love, Hester thought romantically. For Mr Jarvis, the efficient, the alert, the wideawake, to be so absorbed in finding Caroline that he left his wallet behind. Her heart leapt with a strange mixture of emotions.

Then Billie was saying, 'He don't hear, Miss. Come on!' This to his brother. 'Let's go arter him.'

He hastily scooped up the wallet, so hastily that out of it fluttered a square glossy photograph. It landed right side up in front of

Hester. It was of a beautiful dark-haired girl, prettily pouting at the camera.

Unmistakably Miss Clare Phillimore.

CHAPTER SEVEN

To MICK O'ROURKE's disgust, the only winning raffle tickets on Bonnington were held by the two motorcyclists. Johnny and Kenny, the unholy twins, as he had christened them.

'We're not twins, mate,' they told him often enough. 'We live side by side, see. And not in no Irish bog. We're neighbours. Mates.'

A friendly feud had developed between O'Rourke and the boys.

'You look like unholy twins to me. An' now ye've got the luck of the devil.'

'It's not the devil,' Kenny said, 'It's Nurse Stanton. *She* brought us the luck.'

''sright,' Johnny said.

'I did indeed,' Hester laughed, not realising what she was starting. 'I stood right in front of Lady Phillimore yesterday when she drew out the winning tickets. I willed her to get something for Bonnington.'

'Next time, just think of the one name O'Rourke,' Mick said. 'That's the only name that matters.' He had wheeled his chair over between Kenny's and Johnny's bed to inspect their prizes. Johnny had won a radio and Kenny, less appropriately, a bathroom set.

But appropriate or not, both were highly delighted. Neither had won anything before. Not even at ludo. They hoped she hadn't carried them to the hospital on her pedal bike. They were dangerous vehicles, pedal bikes. Worse than horses. They winked at Hester.

'No. My sister dropped them off at the lodge. She drives a Mini.'

'She as pretty as you?'

'Prettier.'

They whistled.

Hester sighed. In a novel, Caroline would just happen to have seen James Jarvis as she left the prizes at the Lodge. But in real life nothing happened. And the fête, after all, had ended in disappointment. Yes, her sister had told her, James came over to her stall. Then the paper boy rushed up with his wallet, and while he was being duly rewarded, Miss Phillimore came to claim him for the drawing of the raffle tickets.

'And who might this Lady Phillimore be?' Mr O'Rourke asked.

'Sir's husband,' Kenny said cheekily.

'The wife of the industrialist,' Hester explained. 'They moved to this area some months ago. They've bought Frantfield Lodge. It's a big house on the south side of the town. He's a great sportsman and a supporter of charity. Their daughter was a patient here for a short time.'

Mr O'Rourke nodded his head knowingly. 'Now I remember, Staff Nurse was after telling me. A beautiful young woman.' He sighed. 'Mr Jarvis' patient, isn't that a fact?'

Hester nodded. 'They were very grateful to Mr Jarvis. Sir Terence gave a big donation to the fête. And,' her voice shook, 'it was announced that he's giving a new orthopaedic wing to the hospital.'

Mr O'Rourke contrived to look impressed and regretful at the same time. Those mixed feelings were much the same as Hester's when the announcement was made yesterday. Mr Jarvis was obviously gratified. He was obviously, also, much approved of by the Phillimore family. And what a suitable marriage for a rising consultant that would be! An indication perhaps of the way the wind was beginning to blow, Miss Phillimore had leaned prettily on her stick and kissed Mr Jarvis impulsively on his cheek. Then she had slipped a hand possessively through his arm till they left the fête together.

Caroline had retired early to bed last night. She had been unusually quiet and sad looking all evening.

'Sure an' you're the quiet one today, Nurse,' Mr O'Rourke said, 'Has that nasty smelly fox cub got your tongue?'

Hester and Sheila Richardson were straightening beds ready for the visiting hours.

'Or has that blind blundering Dr Lewis not been after seeing how pretty you are?'

'Both,' Hester smiled and then the visiting bell sounded. Staff Nurse Mirfield fastened back the ward doors and a tide of visitors swept in. A couple of men in tweed jackets bearing parcels that clinked and gurgled, hailed Mr O'Rourke and straddling the visitors' chairs the wrong way round, began to regale him with reports of various horses' performances at Lingfield.

Sergeant Mounsey, further down the ward, rarely had a visitor and Hester usually made a point of tidying his locker and having a short chat with him.

As she did so that Sunday afternoon, she saw the unholy twins had a visitor who sat between their beds, talking to both of them. She was a pale nervous woman whom Kenny called Mum, and Johnny called Auntie Glad. She was clearly impressed with the radio and the bathroom set, and Nurse's ability to bring good luck.

'You'll be getting her to do your football coupons next,' Kenny's mum suggested hopefully.

The idea was immediately declared a cracker, and visiting hour drifted by as they happily decided how they would spend the lolly when they came up on the treble chance. Kenny was all for blueing some of it on a BSA Goldstar, and Johnny on a three-cylinder Triumph Trident. And both of them were prepared to contribute to a fortnight in Majorca for Mum/Auntie Glad.

'No, it's no good getting me to do those pools things,' Hester said firmly when, two days later, the unholy twins had acquired coupons and invited her active participation. 'I don't know a thing about football.'

'You don't *need* to know one end of the pitch from the other,' Kenny said. 'It's luck that counts.'

'Sure an' they're right, Nurse,' Mr O'Rourke dropped his pretended animosity towards the boys in order to defend luck. 'We Irish respect luck. An' did ye know that Napoleon himself chose his generals for their luck. Ye could at least post the coupons for the lads.'

'Why not?' Peter Lewis said later that week.

He had invited her to supper again at the Horse and Hounds, seeing they both had Wednesday evening off. But this time the evening was blustery and now, having eaten the landlady's grilled trout followed by raspberry cheesecake, they were sitting in a corner of the lounge bar, sipping coffee, and watching the moths fluttering round the lights of the carpark outside.

'It's therapeutic if a patient thinks a nurse is lucky for him. It's like healing hands.' He made that the cue to take her hands in his, 'Small and square and capable,' he smiled, 'dear little hands.' He flicked a glance at her that was oddly serious, almost soulful. 'You see, those lucky lads trust you. You give them confidence. They *like* you.' He smiled shyly, 'I'm getting rather fond of you myself.' He sighed. 'Not that I think you've brought me luck. Far from it. I've had more tickings off from the Boss of late than I've had hot dinners. He doesn't think I've got healing hands. No, sir! He's got his scalpel into me, I can tell you.'

'Miss Phillimore must be getting him down,' Hester said bitterly. 'He swept very smartly in and out of the ward all this week. Hardly seems to see any of the staff.'

'And doesn't he ring to see how Broddi is?'

'No, as a matter of fact he doesn't. But why should he?'

'Ah, yes. Why, indeed. Broddi's off the DI list. Unless of course . . .'

'Unless what?'

'Unless the Boss is interested in another occupant of Honeybourne cottage.'

Hester caught her breath. 'How did you guess?'

'I've told you before, sheer diagnostic skill.' He looked at her affectionately and patted her hand. 'You're a scheming brat, aren't you?'

She shook her head disclaimingly.

'You're trying to spread a little luck in *that* direction too, are you?'

Hester nodded.

'But I warn you, dear Hester, the opposition is stiff.'

'Clare Phillimore?'

'It would seem so. I don't think even Leonie's getting a look in. But there you are. The Boss is very attractive to some.'

'To too many,' Hester said sharply.

'And the course of true love never did run the way scheming brats want it to. So let's not talk about it. Tell me what you're going to do with your day off tomorrow. Then I'll walk you home to your gate. And though I won't come in to inspect Broddi, I will kiss you chastely on the cheek.'

As they walked the short distance back to Honeybourne cottage Hester told him she was going up to London to do some sales shopping, and she had an errand to do for the lucky lads. Reaching the gate, he gave her the promised chaste kiss on her cheek. But suddenly its chastity vanished. He pulled her roughly to him. She was surprised at the strength of his arms, and the urgency with which his lips found hers. She was surprised too at the accomplishment of that kiss, at its warmth and her own sudden response.

'I'm sorry,' he said thickly, finally releasing her. 'Really sorry.' He gave an apologetic laugh. 'You didn't think I had it in me, did you?' He ran his hand through his thatch of yellow hair. 'Surprised myself a bit too, you know.' He sighed, and tilted up her chin. 'Hope I didn't frighten you?'

Hester shook her head.

'Didn't put you off me?'

'No.'

'You see, I felt,' he kissed her again on her parted lips, sweetly this time and very tenderly. 'I strongly felt,' he kissed her again, interspersing his words with little punctuating kisses, 'It was high time . . . I . . . had a share . . . of all this . . . luck . . . that's running around.'

But the luck was running out, even if there had ever been any.

Returning to the ward two days later for early shift, the first thing Hester saw was that the screens were up round young Kenny's bed.

The reasons for the screens were in the night report. Kenny had complained of pains. His temperature and pulse rate had risen. Night Sister had called the SSO and then Mr Jarvis. Lucky young Kenny was to be prepared for theatre.

Peter Lewis came on Bonnington as they were serving lunch. He disappeared behind the screens. He was there a long time. When he emerged he caught Hester's questioning glance and pulled down the corners of his mouth.

'Sister wants you over at Bed 7,' Sheila Richardson whispered, jerking her head towards the screens as Hester pushed the dish trolley away into the corridor. The ward was unusually quiet. And either the catering staff had failed miserably with lunch or everyone was off their food.

Johnny didn't even bother to answer Hester's question, 'Are you sure you can't eat any of this?' as she took away his untouched plate. Nor did he answer her coaxing, 'I thought you liked treacle sponge?'

Even Mr O'Rourke was unsmiling and ominously well behaved.

'Hurry,' Sheila Richardson urged Hester. 'She's in a nit-picker. Kenny's been kicking up a fuss. She reckons you've been got at.'

Sister, Hester reflected wryly, tended to regard it as a reflection on Bonnington's standards of nursing if a patient failed to maintain his unblemished progress. But another matter was displeasing Sister.

She gave Hester a frigid nod as she parted the screens and went behind.

'Now, Kenny,' she said in her brisk nononsense voice to the patient. 'Here is Nurse Stanton. Perhaps we shall now have an end to all this fuss.'

Hester was disturbed by the change in him. Not just the physical change, but a subtle mental one too. Whereas before Kenny and

Johnny had looked like a couple of greasy but jaunty cock sparrows, now he looked bedraggled and defeated. His eyes were dull, his skin flushed. The kidney dish and syringe were on the locker, so Sister had begun the pre-med.

'Does that satisfy you, Kenny?' Sister asked.

In answer, Kenny slowly stretched out his hand towards Hester. After glancing guiltily at Sister, Hester took it. The fingers curled round hers tenaciously. 'Wish me luck?' he asked hoarsely.

'Oh, of course, Kenny. I wish you luck. And by the way,' she tried to force cheerfulness into her voice, 'I posted your coupon.'

Kenny didn't appear to hear.

'Stay with me?' His fingers tightened. 'I'll need your luck. I know I will.'

Usually the pre-med made a patient feel relaxed and cheerful—that much Hester had learned—but to her horror, tears welled up in Kenny's normally bold eyes. He looked a child now in his white theatre gown, and the plastic identification label round his skinny wrist. Hester glanced wide-eyed and questioningly at Sister's tight face. To her astonishment, Sister imperceptibly but quite definitely nodded.

'All right,' Hester said, 'I'll stay with you.'

'All through,' Kenny's speech was becoming slightly blurred but his purpose was unquestionable and clear. '*All* through,' he repeated. 'Don't leave me when I go under. I'll lose me luck if you go. Stay. Say you'll see me through.'

Once again, Hester threw an agonised questioning look at Sister. Again the tiny nod. The small mouth primly pursed, as if Sister didn't really approve of what her head was doing.

'All through,' Hester said as firmly as she could.

Kenny gave a long sobbing sigh. His expression cleared. The pre-med relaxed cheerfulness she had learned about began to take effect.

'I don't like my nurses being got at by patients. And I'm afraid you *have* been,' Sister said, drawing Hester on one side as the theatre porter came to collect Kenny. 'But his state of mind at this juncture is very important.'

'Yes, Sister.'

'If a patient goes in with confidence, he is more likely to come through.'

'There isn't any doubt, is there, Sister. Of him coming through?'

Sister frowned, 'Of course not. He is in very good hands. Now I know you haven't been down to theatre before. So the experience will be very valuable. I have spoken to your tutor and she approves.'

'Yes, Sister.'

'There is no reason why you should do other than take it in your stride. However, if you find you can't, then leave before you make yourself a nuisance. The unforgiveable is to make your-self a nuisance. Remember that.'

'Yes, Sister.' Throwing a glance over her shoulder at the ward, Hester saw Mr O'Rourke put up his thumb. But Johnny was studiously looking the other way.

As they went down in the lift, Kenny, still holding her hand, told the porter, 'She brings me luck.'

'You've got luck all right,' Gainsborough laughed. 'Pretty girl like that to hold your hand. Some lads have it made.'

Between the three of them they kept up a constant chatter. Kenny's responses were slow now, his voice drowsy, his laughter easy to arouse. But surprisingly, as if it had an in-dependent life if its own, his hand held hers. Down the long corridor it slackened a little.

Then they were going through the double doors into the theatre complex. Directly in front of them was a red warning light and the words spelled in illuminated letters, *Operation in Progress*. Kenny raised his head a little, opened his lips as if he'd like to make some jaunty crack and then dropped it back.

Once in the anaesthetic room, his grip on her hand tightened. He eyed the trolley nervously. He released her hand grudgingly for her to don her mask. Then he grabbed it again as she came and stood beside him.

'Sure that's still you?' he asked her suspiciously. 'You look like you're gonna rob the bank.'

'The only robbing we're going to do,' Hester said, trying to make a joke and somehow failing, 'is the pools. Of their prize.'

'Oh, *that*,' Kenny said. 'I don't care about no pools. So long as this is OK. I don't care if I'm skint.' He eyed the robed figure advancing towards him. 'And who's this Herbert? It's not Mr Jarvis. Not unless he's shrunk.'

'The anaesthetist, Kenny.'

'Oh,' Kenny let out a long sigh, as the needle went into his arm.

As he went under, his lips clumsily formed the word 'Stay!'

Hester stayed. At first the complications of donning gown, boots, mask and turban, prevented her thinking too much either of Kenny or what lay ahead.

But once prepared and in the theatre, her heart sank. How would Kenny bear up? How would *she* bear up? Usually students went to theatre in their third year. What if she felt sick? What if she fainted?

The theatre staff were used and prepared for that sort of thing, she knew. There was sal volatile and glucose on hand. But she didn't want to be a hindrance. She most truly wanted to bring Kenny luck.

Nevertheless, the faint rubbery smell, the

heat, the lights, made her head swim. She tried to will everything to be all right for Kenny. He was only a white-draped figure under the lights now, round which anonymous figures bent and moved. At least, all but two were anonymous—the anaesthetist behind the oxygen cylinders, and the tall unmistakable figure of James Jarvis.

As she willed everything to go well she found herself hypnotised by James Jarvis' quiet un-hurried movements, the way he seemed to create around himself an area of harmonious cooperation. A flick of his eye, a hand held out, hardly ever a word said, yet the theatre staff responded.

Time seemed to shrink and expand. Hester felt her mind drift. She was back at the fête watching the bunting-decked platform where Lady Phillimore was drawing out the winning tickets. Then she heard a quiet voice say softly, 'That's it.'

Mr Jarvis straightened. A voice, surely not hers, but from behind her mask asked squeak-ily, 'Is he . . . Did he . . . ?'

But perhaps the voice had neither been hers nor even uttered. Only theatre Sister shot a keen look in her direction, though clearly she heard Mr Jarvis say, 'He'll do.'

A flood of relief made Hester feel weaker still. She wanted to rush over to hug Mr Jarvis. He shot her a penetrating diagnostic look, the

way Sister had done. Then time was doing its
strange expanding and contracting act. Kenny
was being allowed back to the ward. She was
walking beside the stretcher trolley again.
Gainsborough, the porter, seemed to have
everything under control. She remembered
squinting up at the clock on the corridor wall
and seeing that ridiculously, its hands pointed
to four-twenty. Impossible.

'You OK?' Gainsborough asked as they
trundled into the lift. 'Bet you could use a nice
cuppa.' But though her mouth was dry, she
couldn't have swallowed anything.

'You should be off duty now,' Sister said
sternly, helping Sheila Richardson roll Kenny
into bed, but she nodded when Hester asked to
be allowed to stay till Kenny came round.

His first words when he came round and saw
her were, 'Told you I was lucky. Told you I'd
be all right.'

CHAPTER EIGHT

IT SEEMED a long walk down to the bike stand at the far end of the carpark. Her ankles felt rubbery, her feet leaden. Relief made her simultaneously want to laugh and cry, and release from tension made her hands tremble as she tried to wheel out her bike from its concrete rack. The idea of actually mounting it, not to mention riding it through traffic seemed as difficult as a mathematical equation. She was standing uncertainly contemplating the situation, when a deep familiar voice said quietly, 'I think you had better let me deal with that for you, Nurse.' Lean strong fingers fastened over the handlebars. The bike was firmly led over to the open hatch back of Mr Jarvis' familiar white Scimitar and neatly stowed.

'Get in,' Mr Jarvis said, opening the passenger door for her. 'I'll drop you off.' He came and sat in the driver's seat. 'Like that on that bike you'd be a menace to shipping.' He put the key in the ignition and gave her a brief smile.

'But I don't want to take you out of your way,' she said feebly.

'You're not.' He released the brake. 'I was going that way.' And as he released the brake and accelerated out of the carpark, 'You did well this afternoon. I've seen tougher people than you flake out.'

Hester flushed with pleasure.

'Your sister,' he said slowly and softly, 'should be proud of you.'

Emboldened by the meaningful way he said those few and very simple words, Hester suddenly forgot what a poor cupid she made and said daringly, 'Why don't you tell her in person, Mr Jarvis?'

They were heading up the hill from the hospital towards the Honeybourne road. The sun was setting over the distant curve of the Downs. The white chalk quarries gleamed pink.

The traffic was thick and Mr Jarvis kept his eyes studiously ahead, but she studied his profile. There was no doubt that an expression of surprised delight crossed his face. His voice too, when he spoke echoed it. 'I would love to,' he said in a tone she had never heard him use before. 'But Caroline may not be at home.'

'Oh, she will be,' Hester promised. 'She usually comes in for tea at this time. Why not stay, she's always saying she'd love you to come.'

'Really?'

'Really!'

A humorous little quiver momentarily drew together his dark brows. A quirky smile curved his lips. 'Dear Caroline,' he said wistfully.

'So you'll stay for tea?'

'No.' He flicked Hester a glance and actually took one hand off the wheel to pat her arm as if she were some little lap dog, whose yapping he could not pay any attention to. 'Thank you,' he said firmly. 'But no.'

'Are you going somewhere else?' She asked him, suddenly noticing his smart grey suit and the blue silk shirt that turned his eyes to a softer, bluer grey. He was going to meet Miss Phillimore perhaps? Or that old flame in Brighton?

Then his silence made her aware of the impertinence of her question. 'I'm sorry,' she said, 'I shouldn't have asked.'

He didn't reassure her on that point. His foot pressed harder on the accelerator. The traffic thinned. Walls and houses gave way to hedgerows and open fields and dotted woodland. They passed the curve where the fox cub was injured and the crossroads to the chalk quarries. Mr Jarvis seemed totally absorbed in his own thoughts. It was as if he had forgotten all about Hester. His face had taken on a softer, tender look. The look, Hester felt quite certain, of a man suddenly after all these years, delightedly in love.

'Your sister,' Mr Jarvis said sharply as if he

had telepathically been following her train of thought. But he didn't continue, and then she saw he was looking in his driving mirror. The bonnet of a purple Mini had appeared at the Quarry hill crossroads behind them. It tooted, and, happily, Mr Jarvis hooted back.

The purple Mini came squealing out, turning right smartly to follow them at speed.

Mr Jarvis watched the Mini in his driving mirror, while Hester watched him.

It must have been the traumatic experience of the day still affecting her, because she watched the tenderness on his face with a triumph that was edged with almost unbearable pain.

I envy Caroline, she thought, Mr Jarvis is dogmatic, domineering, and unpredictable, a breaker of hearts. Yet if anyone falls in love with me, I hope it will be someone like him and that he will love me like that.

'Your sister drives much too fast,' Mr Jarvis frowned. He took one hand off the wheel and thrusting it through the open window waved her back. 'She worries me,' he frowned, lifting his foot off the accelerator and forcing Caroline to do the same.

'Speak to her about it,' Hester urged, as they glided over Honeybourne bridge. 'Tell her now. She'll take notice of you.'

In answer, Mr Jarvis laughed. She had rarely heard his deep rich laughter, and she was musing to herself on how delightful it sounded, when he said, shaking his head, 'Hester, my dear child, you are the strangest mixture of shyness and persistence. I shall never fathom you.' As he brought the car to a halt, he flicked her a strange puzzled glance as if unable to understand how such a splendid person as Caroline should have a sister like her. 'Do you really want me to come in?'

'Please.'

He spread his hands in a puzzled gesture. Then Caroline was squeaking her brakes to a halt behind them. There was now in the clear light of that summer afternoon, no mistaking that her sister was as delighted to see James Jarvis as he was to see her. Caroline's face was alight. She actually did a Miss Phillimore, and stood on tiptoe to kiss his cheek.

'Dear James!' she said, as if they'd both been on a long journey, as in a way they had, and had at last returned to one another.

'Dear Caroline! This is really just a brief call to tell you not to drive so fast and to tell you that you have a very capable sister.'

He put his hands on her shoulders and kissed her lips. Then they linked arms and walked so naturally together into the cottage.

Hester recognised that the new phase in their closer relationship had begun. That though not for herself, she was still, as Kenny believed, lucky for some.

CHAPTER NINE

THE LUCK of the unholy twins continued. Even
the football coupon which Hester had posted
came up with a modest win of £5.50, a win
which was greeted by the now rapidly recover-
ing boys as if it had been a thousand times that
amount. But the luck did not encompass Peter
Lewis.

Pushing Mr O'Rourke down the corridor to
X-ray, Hester met Peter Lewis coming towards
her with a scowl on his face, even his white coat
somehow flapping disconsolately.

'I suppose you've heard about Mirfield,'
Peter asked her without preamble. As he
only referred to Staff Nurse by her surname
when he was out of favour with her, Hester
guessed, but not having heard anything shook
her head.

'Sure an' I have,' Mr O'Rourke answered for
her.

'So has just about everyone else,' Peter
growled. 'She's got an old flame coming back
from Saudi Arabia. Male of course. Oil en-
gineer. Been making a mint out there. They're
going to whoop it up.'

'Girls will be girls,' Mr O'Rourke said philosophically, enjoying the encounter.

'Whoop it up. Or worse,' Peter went on, hollowly. 'Get married.'

'I don't believe it,' Hester said, 'she's said nothing on the ward. And I must fly. Sister times us.'

'Mirfield's also applied for a job in Saudi,' Peter remarked by way of farewell to the re-treating wheelchair, as if he had to get rid of his frustration somewhere.

'The only reason he's keen on that girl,' Mr O'Rourke explained as they whizzed along to the entrance to X-ray, 'is because she plays hard to get. She's tough. Tougher than Sister. And you can't get tougher than that. If he spent one evening in her company I'd lay a hundred to one on the nose he'd be bored to tears. They're as different as chalk and cheese. He's a nice lad who needs a nice homely girl like you.'

Not, Hester reflected, the most inspiring or cheering of descriptions of herself. Homely was just a little too near plain, too lacking in sparkle, for her liking. And for some reason, which she found difficult to explain, even to herself, life did seem lacking in sparkle. She should, after all, have been feeling particularly happy. The person she loved most in the world, Caroline, was so obviously happy. And her sister's eyes held that particular sparkle that is supposed to come when one is happily in love. Hester herself had helped to bring about that reconciliation with J.J. Why then did she feel this cold emptiness inside herself? Why did she watch her sister's sweet smile as she wrote letters, obviously love letters to James, with the distant melancholy of someone shut out from a warm world which she feels she will never enter? Why did she listen to Caroline going around the cottage humming as she did her chores, with the certainty that she herself would never know the happiness of being loved by the man *she* loved?

By the man she loved. Those were the awful words. For as the days went by and then weeks, she began to admit the terrible suspicion, like some terrible self diagnosis, that she might be in love with J.J. herself.

The symptoms were so obvious and inescapable.

Whenever she saw him, her heart beat quickened and fibrillated like a clock whose mechanism had gone wrong, her mouth dried, her tongue swelled and the palms of her hands became so clammy and trembling that she was afraid to pick up anything that might break.

Thankfully, she saw little of him. She was on night duty. She presumed he was a frequent visitor to the cottage however, for her sister was always preparing intimate little candlelit suppers.

Several times, Hester gathered a mixture of garden and wild flowers and made an arrangement for the table. Returning from one such gathering expedition, with Broddi on the lead, she heard Caroline talking on the phone. 'And I love you, darling,' she heard her say before putting down the receiver. 'Don't worry if you're late. Supper can keep. Come when you're happy about your patient.'

Her sister would, Hester reflected, make the perfect consultant's wife—dedicated, unselfish, loving.

'I thought,' Caroline remarked mistily, watching Hester arranging the last of the roses and some pink chrysanthemums amongst the mauve of Michaelmas daisies, 'as you came in with Broddi, how marvellously,' she stroked the fox's red muzzle tenderly, 'that day changed everything. Changed my whole life. Yours too, perhaps.'

But all Hester could think at that moment, was what a sad smell chrysanthemums have.

There was a sad smell of chrysanthemums in the formal hospital gardens the only time she saw James Jarvis. It was after her last night duty and she was cycling towards the nursing school to check her duties, when his car overtook her. Suffering as she did the usual pangs of clammy hands, dry mouth, trembling limbs and unsynchronised heart movement, she kept her eyes rigidly ahead, concentrating on keeping her wobbling bike as steady as possible. James Jarvis slowed the car, and through the open window called peremptorily, 'Your rear tyre is flat! Get it pumped up. *Now!*'

He watched her in his mirror, till she had dismounted with the clumsiness of someone struggling off an elephant. Then with an angry revving of the engine he zoomed off in his Scimitar.

Two days later, she was helping Peter Lewis put a fresh 'window' dressing on the hip replacement in bed four, when he said, 'Very good, Nurse, you've got a nice neat pair of hands,' and all in the same breath, 'I've got two tickets for the hospital dance, would you do me the honour?'

She accepted with alacrity.

The hospital dance took place in the lecture hall or the nurses' training school, that being the largest room in the hospital complex which was also nicely removed from the wards, where the music of the band would not disturb patients trying to sleep.

The lecture block was surrounded by flower beds and a shrubbery, and that warm September evening, the scent of roses and michaelmas daisies and the sappy smell of laurel leaves mixed again with that sad smell of chrysanthemums.

Perhaps the sad smell warned Hester as Peter drove her up in his old Ford to the carpark in front of the block. A crescent moon had just risen above the tree tops and it was as Peter pointed out, locking the car behind them, a romantic musky night. But already, she knew in her bones, things were not going right.

'That's a pretty dress you're wearing,' Peter said, transferring his gaze from the moon to her bare shoulders, 'Very becoming. That toffee colour suits you. And did anyone ever tell you your waist makes a man ache to put his hands round it?'

He suited his action to his words, and wriggling free Hester said breathlessly, 'My sister made it.'

He laughed. 'The dress, I take it, you mean.'

'Of course,' Hester echoed his laughter more shakily. 'She bought the material in the sales and announced she was going to make it for me.'

'Nice of her,' Peter said politely without much interest. 'She approves, then?'

'Approves? Of what?'

'Of me.'

'She didn't say.' Hester frowned thoughtfully. 'Being on nights I've hardly seen her. She's very busy too. 'So we hardly have time to discuss anything. I was sure she'd come tonight. But . . .'

Peter slid his hand through her arm. 'But what?'

'But she couldn't, she said. She said there

were a couple of patients she wasn't too happy about. Mrs Frith for one, the garage man's wife. She's expecting her fourth and won't go into hospital. Caroline reckons it will be this evening or tonight. Then there's . . .' She broke off.

Peter seemed not to be listening to her. He was listening to the music of the band as it thumped out its seductive rhythm. He took her hand, jived her along the path towards the brightly lit doorway.

But he had been listening more than she had supposed. Just before they pushed open the glass doors into the entrance hall, Peter stopped their rhythmic progress, and put his hands on her bare shoulders. 'So Caroline stayed, like Cinderella, at home?'

'Yes,' Hester answered looking up into his nice blue eyes questioningly.

'And you didn't like that?'

'No.'

'So you, my dear well-meaning, matchmaking Hester, tried to persuade her?'

'I did at first. But of course I couldn't. Not if Mrs Frith . . .' Hester's voice trailed away. A Rolls-Royce, not deigning to take itself to the carpark, had just drawn up directly outside the entrance. The chauffeur got out to open the door. Hester had a glimpse of two familiar heads, one black-haired, short cropped and masculine, the other dark red, exquisitely coiffeured and ultra feminine.

'Come on,' Peter said, hurrying Hester through the entrance, 'let's get in before the VIPs.'

He held open the glass door for her. As she glided in she couldn't resist stealing a glance over her shoulder. James Jarvis, handsome in his dinner jacket, was handing Clare Phillimore from the back of the Rolls. She was dressed in a dark green velvet off-the-shoulder creation. Just before Miss Phillimore stepped down Hester saw her lips brush his unresisting cheek, and she heard her low mellifluous sexy laugh.

'It never pays to look back,' Peter said quizzically. 'Maybe your sister learned that lesson.'

Whether Caroline had learned it or not, Hester had.

She had learned other lessons too, darker and more disturbing. But that evening, she concentrated on that one. She would look forward not back. She would concentrate on the present. The present was the dance, and she danced every number from old-fashioned waltzes and Lancers, for the senior staff, through Lambeth Walks and Congas, Quicksteps and Rumbas, to Rock and Roll and Saturday Night Fever demonstrations. Peter was an expert.

Half way through the last number before the

supper interval, the rest of the dancers smilingly left the floor to them. The band worked itself up to a fever pitch. So did Hester. The electricians, ever ones to enter into the spirit of things, flooded them with vivid jazzy light patterns as they high stepped, waltzed, slid and whirled, till, to a final roll of drums, Peter grabbed Hester round her waist and whirled her off her feet round and round like a catherine wheel. Everyone, from consultants and senior nursing officers downwards, applauded heartily. Everyone that is, except James Jarvis. Hester caught a glimpse of him with his unapplauding arm draped round Miss Phillimore's chair, his eyes intent on her, his head slightly bent to hear the unforgettable words that fell from her lips.

'Phew,' Peter said, draining a long glass of iced fruit cup, 'I feel even hotter than I hope Mirfield will out in Saudi.'

'Is she really going out there?'

'So rumour hath it.'

'But you've heard no more.'

'No.'

'Do you mind?' Hester asked gently. She was beginning to feel a deep empathy with all star-crossed lovers.

'Why should I? Girls like Mirfield aren't really my cup of tea.' He shrugged. It was the nearest he came to talking about Leonie. There was no sign of her at the dance. She was certainly not on duty. Sister was on in Bonnington till the night staff took over. 'I prefer to see to my patients than dance the light fantastic,' she had told her nurses with a prim and wintry smile.

But the dance was full of familiar faces. When the band resumed after the supper interval, it was with a Paul Jones. Under the bright lights, Hester watched the familiar faces almost merge as the music whirled them faster, the elderly porter at the gate, merging with the new path. lab. boy, the portly chief accountant merging with Dr Salmon the anaesthetist, till she could hardly distinguish one from the other. Then, at its crescendo, the music stopped, and there opposite her, clear cut and inescapable, was James Jarvis.

One moment, she was rooted to the spot. The next she was floating in his arms. For one delirious second, it seemed the most natural place in the world to be. She had the most absurd desire to rest her head against his broad chest, to let her whole being somehow melt into his. She was acutely aware of his hand in the small of her back, of his breath lightly fanning her hair. But swiftly the familiar symptoms took over. Her mouth went dry, her legs seemed to vanish, her heart broke into a frightening rhythm.

Then, like a therapeutic slap across her face, or a dash of cold water, this man who caused it

all held her a little away from him and said in a
cool, rather contemptuous voice, his eyes
stern, 'You seem to have been making quite a
surprising exhibition of yourself.'

A flood of anger tautened Hester's whole
being. She felt the indignant colour heighten
in her cheeks. She thought of her sister
Cinderella-like at home, while he flaunted
himself with Miss Phillimore. Her eyes spark-
led. She heard a voice she could hardly recognise as her own reply, unforgivably, 'Then I am
not the only one, am I?'

Mercifully, the band began its whirling
rhythm again. Dancing partnerships were dissolved, as once more the male and female
circles formed up.

Lest those circles brought her face to face
with James Jarvis again, Hester disentangled
herself, and, escaping from the dance floor,
walked out through the open entrance doors.
She stood for a moment at the top of the three
steps, drawing in the cool softly scented night
air, till her body stopped shaking and her heart
beat quietened.

She heard Peter's voice behind her. 'What a
good idea, Hester. It's baking hot in there.' He
slid his arm round her waist. 'Let's go for a
stroll.'

It began as a stroll and a gentle, relaxed,
friendly one at that.

It continued as a rather comic dance. The music leaked out of the open windows, and even as far as the carpark. They executed little steps together, across the half-empty carpark and down the paths. It was, as Peter pointed out, cool and uncrowded, and the crescent moon was now high above.

It ended as they began to retrace their footsteps back towards the dance. Half way there, Peter drew her onto a small wooden seat facing the statue of the hospital founder. 'I want to talk to you,' he said urgently, and she turned to him questioningly, suddenly he pulled her to him, and kissed her parted lips with a rough demanding ardour that seemed natural, unfeigned, and to which she found herself beginning to respond. Even as she did so she knew it wasn't as it seemed. It was in response not to him, but to something deep and hurtful inside herself. Something that kissing Peter helped to drive out. Some deep hunger that his kisses momentarily assuaged. Perhaps his passion, too, was in response to something similar. Whatever it was, he began tightening one arm round her and kissed her throat, while his other hand cupped her breast.

Immediately, she came to her senses. She tried to push his hand away, and wriggled to escape his clasp. But her struggles only made him tighten his grip.

'Please!' she began, but determinedly his

mouth found hers again. She turned her head from side to side, squirmed her body in his grasp. But he laughed in a frightening, unfamiliar, almost exultant way. Freeing a foot from her long skirt she kicked out, but though she felt her high heel make contact, his grip didn't slacken.

Then suddenly a hand descended on each of their shoulders. A hand whose grip was as hard as Peter's but which grasped her without any desire or any emotion except anger. Peter took one guilty glance behind him and then struggled to his feet.

James Jarvis towered above the pair of them. The only cause Hester had for thankfulness was that at least he was alone.

'I'll speak to you in the morning,' he said curtly to Peter. 'Come and see me then. Eight-thirty. We've a busy day. I suggest you turn in. *I* shall see Hester gets home.' He dismissed Peter with a peremptory nod of his head. And with a little apologetic spread of his hands, Peter went.

'It was my fault as well,' Hester said.

'I had already supposed that to be the case,' James Jarvis replied evenly.

'And anyway . . .' she stopped abruptly. A torrent of unsayable words, phrases, reproaches, self-justification pressed to flood out. Reproaches about her sister Cinderella-like at home, about J.J.'s duplicity, about

Peter's relative innocence, were held back only by her determinedly clamped teeth.

'And anyway *what*?' James Jarvis demanded tersely.

Something in his expression forbade her to continue. 'And anyway,' she said thickly, 'you don't need to take me home.'

He gave her a thin smile. 'I didn't say *I* would take you home,' he said icily, 'I said I would see you got home.' He raised one eyebrow derisively. 'I suggest you gather your things. Meanwhile I'll get the lodge to send round a taxi.'

The last glimpse Hester had that night of James Jarvis was through the dance hall windows, as she climbed into the taxi. He was waltzing cheek to cheek with Miss Phillimore, while Hester, though she didn't cry all the way home, certainly she wiped her eyes at very frequent intervals.

She found the cottage empty. A note in her sister's handwriting on the kitchen table headed 9.30, read, 'I was right about Mrs Frith. Don't expect me back till the wee hours. Sorry I couldn't finish washing up.'

The strange thing was that though James Jarvis had been very obviously at the dance, there were two of everything in the sink, two meat plates, two dessert bowls. Someone had shared her sister's late supper.

Her Cinderella sister had not dined alone.

CHAPTER TEN

WHEN Sister held 'Report' five days later, she was not alone. She had sitting beside her a thick-set bronzed man of about thirty in white trousers and short sleeved smock top, whom she introduced as Charge Nurse Grant.

'Charge Nurse Grant will be taking over from Staff Nurse Mirfield,' she announced, and when Hester opened her mouth in an involuntary exclamation, she demanded severely, 'Yes, Nurse Stanton? Did you wish to make some comment?'

'No, Sister. It's just that . . . well . . . I'd heard . . .'

As Sister cleared her throat to give her usual little lecture on nurses being got at by gossip, Charge Nurse spoke.

'I reckon most of us had heard something of Staff Nurse's new job,' Charge Nurse Grant had a slight Australian accent. He gave Hester a brief smile, 'And we wish her well. You'll find my ways much the same as hers. But I've got a few more muscles,' he flexed his right arm humorously, and Sheila Richardson let out a hungry admiring sigh, happily only heard by Hester.

'It's heavy work,' Charge Nurse Grant went on in that slow drawl, 'restraining men like Mr O'Rourke, and turning poor old chaps like Sergeant Mounsey.'

At the mention of Mr O'Rourke Sister gave her usual exasperated frown, but her face cleared at the mention of the old Sergeant.

'Which reminds me,' she said as 'Report' came to an end. 'The Sergeant has a birthday.' She flipped through the Kardex to check. 'Yes. next Monday. A most important birthday. Eight-five. I'll warn the Catering Officer about the cake. Who's on duty next Monday after-noon?'

Hester and Sheila Richardson put up their hands. So did the Australian.

'And how about a whip-round for a pres-ent?' Charge Nurse Grant suggested.

'We—ell . . .' A cake for patients having a birthday was common practice at the Frantfield and District, but a whip-round for a present was another matter. Sister, ever meticulously correct, hesitated.

'There's no rule against it,' said the Austra-lian.

'No.'

'And you said he'd got no one,' the Austra-lian went on.

'True.'

'And the ex-Serviceman's home he's in can't cope with him till he's fully mobile. And heaven knows when that'll be.'

Sister said nothing for several moments. Then primly she dipped into her pocket, brought out her purse, unclasped it and took out a pound note. 'I'll start it off,' she said. 'Nurse Stanton being the most junior can collect while Sergeant Mounsey is asleep.'

These days, the poor old Sergeant was increasingly asleep, so it wasn't difficult for Hester to make her collection. In fact the only difficulty was to restrict enthusiasts like Mick O'Rourke from giving too much.

'Upward limit of 50p per patient,' Hester said firmly to him.

'Fifty pence a pig's eye!' he exclaimed.

'No arguing, Mr O'Rourke. Sister's orders!'

'Faith an' you're getting a hard one,' Mr O'Rourke said, stuffing his five pound note back in his pyjama pocket. 'You'll get as hard as Sister one day, I shouldn't wonder.'

'We only want to buy him a new tobacco pouch—That old one of his is falling apart—and some flowers.' Hester popped his thermometer in Mr O'Rourke's mouth, and lifted his wrist. 'Just a token.'

'He's a grand old man,' Mick O'Rourke sighed sentimentally when he was free to talk again. 'Eighty-five. I hope I'll do as well.'

Across the ward, Kenny and Johnny shook their heads and put down their thumbs. Mr O'Rourke pretended to shake his fist in reply.

But the hostility these days was more of an act than reality. They still fiercely argued the merits of horse riding and motorcycling. Mr O'Rourke turned up his nose at their queer jargon as they did at his. 'Going for a scratch means doing a ton, a fast ride,' they told him. 'Not like you reckon, an old nag rubbing itself on a tree stump.'

'Are you getting someone to come in and see the old codger?' the boys asked Hester on the Sunday when she was rolling them over to powder their backs.

Hester nodded. 'They're bringing his friend from the Legion Home. So it will be quite a little party.'

'Iced birthday cake and lemonade,' Kenny sniffed with pretended derision.

'Sure an' I'd have some champagne brought in,' Mr O'Rourke whispered on Monday morning as Peter Lewis watched Hester change his dressing, 'but the Boss would shoot me, wouldn't he?'

'He wouldn't even wait for dawn,' Peter assured him drily.

'And how are you after liking Charge Nurse Grant instead of Staff Nurse Mirfield, Doctor?' Mr O'Rourke asked him slyly.

Peter Lewis busied himself with balancing Mr O'Rourke's weights and ignored the question.

It was however a question that few other

people ignored. It was the general consensus of opinion amongst the nurses of Bonnington that Bill Grant was a vast improvement. Sheila Richardson had found out that he wasn't married, though he was reported to have a girl friend. He lived in modest lodgings in the town and spent most of his free time playing squash, though he too liked collecting records. He was popular with the patients, with the exception of Mr O'Rourke who said he had a rough pair of hands that would ruin a horse's mouth and didn't do much for his clavicle. Kenny and Johnny liked him enormously. He was second only to J.J. in their estimation.

Of James Jarvis, Hester had seen little. Her sister still seemed happy and in love. She had helped Hester choose the tobacco pouch, which was now wrapped ready in Sister's office, with the flowers and the cards.

No one all that day made any mention that they knew it was Sergeant Mounsey's birthday. Though to Hester's perhaps over-imaginative eye he seemed to look hopeful and then hopeless as the mail was distributed.

Then at 2 p.m. visiting hour began. The warden of Sergeant Mounsey's home came in with a white-haired wispy gentleman, whom O'Rourke said was the Sergeant's best friend. The warden carried a square brown paper parcel which Mr O'Rourke bet was cigars, and the wispy gentleman a smaller box which

O'Rourke said was chocolate mints.

O'Rourke's horsy friends had let him down because there was a race meeting that afternoon, so he was without visitors, and spent the time watching Sergeant Mounsey's delight. The *pièce de résistance* was, however, after the end-of-visiting bell had sounded. Sergeant Mounsey's visitors had been told they could stay. Then cards and presents were produced. The cake was wheeled in, its eight-and-a-half candles lit. As the nursing staff gathered round Sergeant Mounsey's bed, a tall figure quietly opened the ward doors and walked unobtrusively in. He was dressed in a sports coat and twill trousers. He came and stood behind Hester.

'Help me cut it, Nurse Hester, there's a duck,' Sergeant Mounsey was saying, his plump face wreathed in smiles.

'Help him,' the newcomer echoed, and recognising the voice, Hester turned sharply. James Jarvis had joined the party. And in party mood, he lifted her hand and leaning forward placed it over the old man's.

'Sure an' it's like the cutting of a wedding cake,' Mr O'Rourke remarked mistily.

'Well it's the happiest day I've had for many a year,' the old Sergeant said.

If he had felt the trembling of Hester's hand he was old enough and wise enough not to remark on it, and understanding enough to squeeze hers gently and reassuringly. The cake was cut and distributed round the ward. So were the cigars and the chocolate mints.

Then at four the party dissolved. Mr Jarvis shook the old Sergeant's hand and took his leave. Five minutes later, glancing out of the ward window, Hester saw the surgeon get into a small open sports car driven by a girl with flowing red hair.

But she had not many days to mourn the duplicity of James Jarvis towards her sister. The following Thursday night, Sergeant Mounsey died quietly in his sleep. And the most urgent problem on her mind became not to let Sister see the slightest sign of grief.

'It's part of what you have to learn,' Caroline said gently the next evening. 'How to cope with grief. Your own and other people's. That's one of the things you're trained for.'

As she spoke, Caroline bent down and gently stroked Broddi as she lay at her feet. The fox cub let out a little muted churring sound like a cat greeting its mistress. 'You've got to care. But learn not to care too much. Life's difficult. And full of contradictions.'

'Sister is full of contradictions too,' Hester sighed. 'She was furious with Richardson because she said she heard her what she called snivelling. But she was very sweet to Kenny and Johnny. She told them they were right to mourn such a fine old man.'

'There's always one law for patients and another for nurses.'

'Yet she was very sharp with Mr O'Rourke. Told *him* not to be so sentimental. But then she always is sharp with Mr O'Rourke.'

'Poor Sister, I wonder why?'

Hester shrugged. 'She reckons he flirts with the nurses.'

'She's probably right.'

'And that he gossips.' Hester stopped herself and frowned. One of Mr O'Rourke's pieces of gossip had been about James Jarvis and Miss Phillimore. But as if her sister had read her mind, she asked with a casualness that did not quite ring true, 'Have you seen much of James Jarvis?'

'Hardly anything.'

'I've seen him several times,' Caroline suddenly volunteered.

Hester held her breath and said nothing. A small introspective smile curved her sister's lips as if momentous and happy news hovered there, waiting only for the right moment to be said.

Caroline sighed. She must have decided the time was almost but not quite ripe for she suddenly asked softly, and confidentially, 'Do you like him, Hester?'

For some reason Hester's cheeks flamed. 'Of course I like him,' she answered hoarsely. 'You like him very much, don't you?'

'More than like him,' her sister said softly.
She stretched out her hand and covered
Hester's.

'Love him?' Hester croaked, feeling now she
must grasp this painful piercing nettle. 'Do you
love him?'

Caroline gave her low attractive happy
laugh. 'Well, not in the way a young girl means
love.'

'What way, then?' Hester breathed.

'Oh, how can I put it?' Caroline held her
head on one side.

'I don't know,' Hester said miserably.

Now that the nettle was almost in her hand
she was afraid of how much it would hurt. She
wanted to clap her hands over her ears, so as
not to hear the fatal words, 'I love him as a
mature woman loves a man.'

But it was the fox's ears that suddenly dis-
tracted her sister's attention. She jumped to
her feet, ears pricked.

'Now who can she hear that we can't,'
Caroline asked, a faint flush stealing under her
skin.

'Expecting anyone?' Hester asked.

'Not really,' her sister looked at her watch.

'A patient?'

Her sister shook her head. Then stood up
and began plumping the cushions of the sofa.
'James Jarvis,' Hester said but not aloud, and

simultaneously the front door bell sounded peremptorily.

'Ask whoever it is in for a sherry,' her sister said, her eyes bright, as Hester, followed by Broddi walked towards the front door.

Broddi was sniffing and making little dog-like whining noises of pleasure as if he knew whoever it was on the other side of the door.

Hester took a long time turning the key in the lock, because once again, her hands trembled, and her limbs felt weak.

When she threw the door open the tall figure wasn't James Jarvis at all. Hester stood for several seconds staring at the burly shape of Alistair Matherson, the vet, while mingled relief for herself and disappointment for her sister washed over her like the hot and cold of a fever.

'Sorry if I frightened you, Hester dear,' he said in his slow countryman's voice, a puzzled expression crossing his brows. 'I was just passing by and thought I'd seen how young Broddi here . . .' his voice broke off in a cry of warning, 'Hey, hold her!' He made a sudden grab, but with a quick twist Broddi eluded him, and went streaking down the garden path.

Hester's shriek brought Caroline to the door. They both saw the fox clear the gate at a single leap, despite her damaged leg.

Then, deaf to their cries, she was off up the High Street towards the bright October woods.

CHAPTER ELEVEN

'IT WAS all my stupid fault. There I stood, rooted to the spot, while Broddi slipped past me,' Hester told Peter Lewis over lunch at the Horse and Hounds two days later.

The fox's escape had acted as peacemaker between them.

'Just as, dearest Hester, it was all my stupid fault at the dance.' Peter stretched his hand across the table and touched hers. 'I'd been working like a slave, I'd not eaten all day. Yes, I know what you're going to say, you've warned me often enough. Then I'd had two glasses of famous Nurses' Home fruit punch. Fatal!' He smiled his boyish, disarming smile. 'One gets carried away. One forgets oneself. You're sorry about Broddi. And I'm sorry, most deeply frightfully sorry to embarrass you in front of the Boss.'

'Oh, you didn't really.'

'Well you looked embarrassed. You went red as a turkey and then as white as a bed sheet.'

'Did he say much to you next morning?'

'Just rapped my knuckles.'

'Hard?'

'Broke the skin in places,' he laughed rue-fully. 'You know the Boss when he's on his high-minded horse—' Peter broke off, and said suddenly, 'He's really fond of your sister, isn't he?'

'Yes. I think so.'

'I know so,' he nodded sagely. 'Well, he went on a bit about young impressionable girls in general, and ungentlemanly behaviour in par-ticular. About how well your sister had tried to bring you up till now. What a disappointment such behaviour would be. I said I was sorry and it wouldn't happen again. At least I meant not until you wanted me to. Kiss you, I mean. Etcetera. Though I didn't tell him that, natur-ally. In the meantime,' he squeezed her hand, 'all I can do is help you look for Broddi.'

Peter had reinstated himself in Hester's re-gard by his genuine concern about the fate of the fox, and the warmth with which he had espoused the cause of finding her. 'With a bit of string-pulling here and a bit of swapping there, I can get my half day off at the same time as yours.'

Hester would have preferred to start the search immediately they left the hospital, but Peter was adamant that these days he had learned the lesson of not skipping meals, and had insisted on stoking up first on platefuls of Mrs Latter's beefsteak pie and garden greens. He had spent much of the lunch time, true, on asking the locals in the bar if they'd seen Broddi, but the locals had already been alerted by Hester and Caroline. Indeed the postman had had a sighting the previous afternoon of a fox with a slight limp, making across a stubble field towards the chalk quarries on the Downs.

Following that telephone clue Caroline had taken the Mini on to the Downs at dawn but she had seen nothing.

'You see, she could hardly have escaped at a worse time,' Hester said, watching Peter mop the last of the gravy with one of Mrs Latter's home-baked rolls. 'On Saturday week, the Frantfield Foxhounds Hunt begins with a cubbing.'

'And what's that?'

'Killing the fox cubs. If they get scent of Broddi she won't stand a chance.'

'Don't worry,' Peter pulled her to her feet. 'Don't cross your bridges till you come to them. We'll find her.'

But they didn't. All that autumn afternoon, they tramped through woods, across fields and meadows, crossed half a dozen bridges and forded as many downland streams. They called. They put down little enticing morsels of her favourite minced chicken and mushroom skins and lumps of cheese to which she was very partial. They enquired at farmhouses, where some farmers' wives were sympathetic, but others with protective eyes on their chickens promised they'd shoot the red devil on sight if they did see her.

Till as the sun was beginning to sink, Peter flung himself on the bracken and pronounced himself exhausted. 'Sit down, Hester. Rest your weary limbs.' He patted the bracken invitingly. 'If I put my arm behind your head, you won't feel the prickles. Use me,' he said magnanimously, 'as your pillow.'

Hester hesitated. Then sat down primly, clasping her knees.

'Come on. Take it easy. No kissing, etcetera. I promise.'

Gingerly she lay back with her head resting on his outflung arm, her eyes staring up at the now rosy sky above.

'You see, I want to give you a demonstration of how well I keep my promise.'

The demonstration was not to be. From the ash woods just across the dip of the valley came the unmistakable screeching bark of a young vixen. They sat up simultaneously in time to see a minute copper streak flicker out into the open, in and out of the bracken paths and then turn in the approximate direction of Honeybourne.

'We thought she might be heading for home,' Hester told her sister that night.

Not surprisingly, under the circumstances, Alistair Matherson was there.

They'd just had high tea and were enjoying the last cup by the log fire in the sittingroom.

'I feel far more to blame than Hester,' he had kept saying. 'I startled the poor girl. She was obviously expecting her boy friend.' And on that he had refused to be contradicted. He had also refused to be left out of the search. Now, with his hands thrust into the pockets of his baggy tweed jacket, he stood with his back to the log fire, listening to Hester.

'Are you certain it was Broddi?'

'As certain as one can be at that distance.'

'Did you call to her?'

'Till we were hoarse.'

'We, I take it, is the boy friend and you.'

'Peter? Well, he's . . '

'One of several,' her sister said inaccurately and somewhat surprisingly. 'A nice enough boy, but . . .'

Alistair laughed. 'Spare me,' he said, 'from ever being "nice enough, but . . ."'

They all laughed, and in his easy natural way, Alistair guided the subject back to Broddi. 'In my opinion she's not quite ready to survive on her own in the wild. But she'll be all right for a day or so. Her leg slows her, but not badly. And this time of the year there are berries and insects and fungus if she can't catch anything else.'

'I was speaking to James today,' Caroline said, glancing at Hester and that faint telltale colour coming up under her skin. 'He said that Broddi knew best. The time had come.'

Alistair patted his pockets to find his pipe, brought it out, filled it slowly, packing the tobacco down with care, then, lighting it, he drew in long thoughtful puffs. 'Well,' he said judiciously after all that, 'James is entitled to his opinion.'

How much nicer and tolerant, Hester thought, are vets than doctors, how much more kindly and human.

'He probably said that to tease you, Caroline,' Alistair went on.

'Probably,' her sister agreed, her eyes on Hester. 'He also said young foxes were like young humans. They needed to learn by their mistakes.'

'Oh,' Hester exclaimed, her cheeks crimson, 'Did he also tell you . . . ?' But no, surely even J.J. didn't tell tales out of school. Once again Alistair turned the conversation back to Broddi.

'But when the weather gets colder, then I doubt she'll survive. And most pressing of all, the Hunt. In hunt rules they're not supposed to hunt an animal that's been handled. The devil of it is to stop the hounds once they've got the scent. If they do, she'll never outstrip the dogs with that leg. She won't have a snowball's chance in hell.'

Pausing for a dozen puffs of his pipe to let that sink in Alistair continued, 'I've given this some careful thought.'

'I know you have,' Caroline said warmly. 'And it's sweet of you.'

'No more than I ought,' Alistair growled. 'Not one bit more, that is so. And even that thinking hasn't given me much in return. Except this. If we can't find Broddi before the Hunt, how about getting the Hunt to postpone its first cubbing?'

'Do you think they might?' Hester brightened.

'I think they well might. They're reasonable people. They want to give the fox a chance. We can remind them of the rules. They don't want to hunt a three-legged animal. It's not sporting. The MFH is a very sporting fellow, I'm told. And if the right person asked him . . .'

'You?' Hester suggested smiling.

Alistair shook his head. 'A pretty charming and attractive person I had in mind.'

'Caroline.'

'No, Hester. *You.*'

'Oh,' Hester let out a long reluctant sigh. 'And who is the MFH I'm supposed to see?'

'As I said,' Alistair beamed cheerfully, 'a very sporting fellow. A very charitable man. Well-known he should be to you. Sir Terence Phillimore. The donor of the new orthopaedic unit.'

'I know.' Hester let out an even longer sigh.
'And the father of Clare.'

The father of Clare was not alone, when he
reluctantly granted Hester an interview with
him. He had suggested that if she really must
see him so urgently, then she should come to
Frantfield Lodge punctually at 5 o'clock on
Thursday afternoon, which was the only time
he could offer her.

Frantfield Lodge was the grandest house
Hester had ever approached. It was set on the
outskirts of Frantfield Wells, about two and a
half miles from the hospital, whence she had
cycled with anxious speed.

Early shift at the Sussex and District ended
at four-thirty. But as Sister Bonnington frequently said, 'While punctuality in reporting
for duty is imperative, punctuality in reporting
off duty is not to be recommended.'

She had pursed her lips disapprovingly as
Hester donned her cape and fled. She would
like to have changed from her uniform before
meeting Sir Terence, but time pressed.

Thursday afternoon, as it was, left less than
forty-eight hours before the cubbing, and Sir
Terence, she had been told, was not the kind of
man to be kept waiting.

Glancing at her watch as she cycled through
the huge open gates, she saw she had exactly
five minutes to spare. The drive curved on

either side of a lawn planted with a tall monkey puzzle tree, and beyond it, on a slight rise, a lovely Queen Anne house, its rows of matched windows rosy in the rays of the setting sun.

Drawn up in front of the house were several cars, a Rolls-Royce, a Range Rover and the sporty little car Hester had seen James Jarvis climb into after poor old Sergeant Mounsey's birthday party. Hester dismounted and rested her bike against the stone balustrade, at a suitably modest distance.

She climbed the impressive stone staircase, but before she had time to sort out which was the front door bell, the door opened, and a bald disapproving man, who was obviously the butler, bade her good afternoon and invited her to come inside.

'Sir Terence is expecting you. Your vehicle is I hope safely parked . . . ?' He peered over her shoulder.

'Perfectly, thank you.'

A silver clock with a note like its exquisite face was just chiming the hour. A deeper-voiced grandfather clock echoed the chimes from the shadowy recesses of the vast hall.

'If you would follow me to the library,' the butler inclined his head and began walking with measured tread across the hall and down a corridor hung with tapestries, till he came to a door almost at the far end, where he tapped discreetly and listened.

'Come!' a testy voice snapped in reply. 'It's one minute past.'

After the testy tone came a familiar low mellifluous laugh, and when the butler opened the door Hester saw Clare, sitting gracefully on a corner of her father's desk. She was wearing a dress of some chiffony material in a very becoming shade of apricot, her hair was scooped back in a matching bandanna, her shapely legs were crossed, and she wore thin strappy sandals in exactly the same shade of apricot on her feet.

Behind such a bright bird of paradise, Sir Terence grey-haired and dressed in a grey suit of impeccable and conservative cut, looked colourless and almost harmless.

Till you saw the gleam in his sharp brown eyes and the purply colour beneath his well-shaved skin. And till he spoke.

'It's no good coming in your Florence Nightingale get-up. You'll get no more out of me that way.'

'Oh, I know. I didn't mean to come like this. I hadn't the time to change.'

'There's always time if you make time,' he said grittily. 'If you were going out with some young man you'd change wouldn't you?'

'Of course she would!' Clare answered for her. 'She's that young nurse . . .' she bent across the desk to whisper in her father's ear. Hester caught the name 'James', and the word 'dance'. Her face flushed.

'Well,' Sir Terence said judicially, 'That's none of our business. Now don't waste any more of my time, Nurse, what exactly did you want to see me about?'

Haltingly, Hester began.

'Well, sit down, young lady. Especially if it's going to be a long story, which I fear it is.'

And then as she got half way through, 'Always remember, young lady, the best stories are the short ones.'

But he heard her out. From the finding of the fox, through the rearing of it, how Alistair had said it was not yet ready to cope with the wild, to its escape and her final request that the cubbing be postponed. Clare too, followed her every word with bright-eyed hostile intent.

At the word 'postponed', Clare jumped off the desk in righteous anger. She stamped one of those lovely apricot sandals and exclaimed, 'But I'm so looking forward to it. It's my first ride since my op. You can't cancel, Daddy. You shan't. Remember we're giving the Hunt breakfast. And I've got everything new. Besides James . . .'

She flung her arm round her father's shoulder and whispered in his ear again.

This time she heard something about that stupid sentimental vet, and Sir Terence's reply with indulgent protest, 'Oh, he's quite a good fellah, m'dear. Widower, and all that. Manages very well. Did a splendid job when Princess foaled.'

Balked of attacking Alistair, Clare pouted, then returned to whispering in her father's ear. She kept her voice discreetly low till carried away by her own emotion, the words, 'that wretched District Nurse or whatever she is,' came over loud and clear.

And as Hester opened her mouth to protest, Sir Terence said, 'Pretend you didn't hear that!'

'Besides James says . . .'

'No, darling,' Sir Terence patted his daughter's hand, 'I think you've said enough. I've heard this young lady's side, and now I've heard yours.' He looked at his watch. 'It is almost fifteen after five and I shall now give you my decision.'

'I need to say more,' Hester pleaded. 'According to your rules, it's very unsporting to hunt a lame fox.'

Smiling slyly without humour, Clare answered, 'Foxes are like humans, they need to learn by their mistakes.'

James Jarvis' very words, Hester reflected bitterly. Her thoughts were interrupted by Sir Terence ringing a bell on his desk, and as if he had been waiting on the other side of the door, the butler appeared.

'My decision, young lady, is that the cubbing

cannot be postponed. Wainwright, kindly show this young lady to the door.'

Cheeks flaming with anger and embarrassment, Hester followed the butler to the front door. In the fifteen minutes she had been allowed inside, a Scimitar had drawn up beside the Rolls. Its driver had got out, and was now inspecting her bike. He was tall, dark-haired and though dressed in blue-grey country tweeds, unmistakably James Jarvis. As she came down the steps he actually had the temerity to put his hands on the handlebars and wheel it a few yards. Till that moment she hadn't realised how complicated were her feelings towards him. Now what she feared was love, real passionate unassuageable love, not the mature love her sister had spoken of, was mixed so inextricably with an equally passionate and unassailable hatred. Questions seethed in her mind. How could Caroline love such a man so blindly and compliantly, even if that love went under the name of mature? Why did he, the object of such love, dance attendance on such a hard frivolous girl as Clare? And why was he here now, for instance?

He didn't turn as she scrunched her feet angrily across the gravel of the forecourt. Yet he seemed to know it was she who stood beside him and not to be in the least embarrassed.

'At least you got that tyre pumped up,' he said equably by way of greeting. 'But I don't like the look of that chain. The whole contraption needs a good overhaul.'

And as she began, 'It's none of your . . .' he went on smoothly, 'So what brought you here? Broddi? A wasted journey! I could have told you.'

Eyes sparkling with anger, she retorted, 'Why didn't you tell them?'

'And what should I tell them?' He frowned down at her, his brows drawn together, his own eyes challenging. 'That they must do what you want them to?'

'Well, not that foxes are like human beings and have to learn by their mistakes.'

She recognised that they were both now angry with each other. J.J. in a controlled way and herself much less controlled. So much less that she had completely forgotten that he was a consultant and she a humble student nurse.

'I'm glad at least,' J.J. drawled, 'that my words have become apocryphal. That Clare remembered them. Or was it Caroline?'

That was all too much for Hester. Such cold-blooded coupling together of the two women.

She stamped her foot in a way that would have done Clare credit. 'Both of them,' she replied. 'Both of them!' she reiterated. 'I've had it from both of them. I hate you! I hate you!' She sobbed. 'For what you're doing to Caroline.'

Then she snatched her bike, mounted it at a run and went wobbling off down the drive. But really she knew she meant, 'I hate you for what you're doing to me!'

CHAPTER TWELVE

ON THE Saturday of the cubbing, Hester was on early shift. She left the cottage at seven on a fine crisp morning. A good hunting morning with the air still and clear as isinglass to preserve the scent of the quarry. The woodland trees had not yet lost their leaves, and the great heads of Sussex oak and beech and elm stood out golden and russet against a paling sky. The hedgerows were thick with blackberries and rosehips and crimson trails of convolvulus berries, the twigs netted with small spiders' webs sparkling with dew. But Hester saw little of the morning's beauty. Somewhere, deep in that coppery wood, a figure that matched its colour probably hurried about its unlawful business blissfully unaware of the dangers that awaited her.

'She'll have a sixth sense about it,' Alistair had said last night. 'Besides, foxes have trails and recognition posts. They give each other information. She'll know the hunting horn spells danger. She'll go to ground. She'll lie low.'

'But where will she lie?' Hester had asked. 'She's got no earth.'

'She'll find somewhere,' Alistair had puffed his pipe contently and sounded confident. 'Foxes can live in caves, burrows or trees. They can live on fungi and insects. The woods are full of hiding places.'

Several times that morning, Hester heard a rustling behind the hedgerows. She dismounted and called. But it was only a rabbit or a squirrel, or a blackbird searching for worms.

And then arriving at Bonnington, all thoughts of Broddi were momentarily erased from her mind.

Immediately after 'Report', as she was about to wheel the breakfast trolley into the ward, Charge Nurse Grant announced, with the cheerfulness of someone who bears unwelcome news, 'Hope your hands are good and steady this morning. Orders from PTS. I'm to give you your stitches assessment.'

Sheila Richardson pulled a sympathetic face. 'It comes to us all sooner or later, ducks.'

Then, as they made Mr O'Rourke's bed and tidied his well-stocked locker, Richardson added, 'Anyway you're lucky to have someone like Bill Grant to supervise you. *I* had Sister.'

'Sister's a hard woman,' Mr O'Rourke, who couldn't keep out of any conversation, however whispered, sighed.

'Bill on the other hand is kind, relaxed, reassuring, has a wonderful ear for music, and . . .'

'And is engaged to be married,' a voice behind them said. Peter Lewis had come softly into the ward. He stood with his hands in his trouser pockets, smiling teasingly at Sheila Richardson's blushes.

'I hear there's an important assessment at eleven,' he turned to Hester, and put up his thumb. 'I thought I'd take a glance. Act as referee, in case of dispute. Give resuscitation to the patient or the nurse if necessary.'

He laughed at Hester's expression. 'Fear not. It isn't your assessment I'm concerned with. But whether your victim, Mr Wilkinson, can be discharged. Meanwhile the Boss wants me to have a word, indeed several words with the twins.' He smiled. 'On the importance of wearing skid-lids, as those two call them.' And in the same breath, 'No news of Broddi, I suppose?'

Hester shook her head.

'And the cubbing meet goes on?'

'Yes, I failed miserably with Sir Terence. He didn't take to me. He was quite adamant. That was that.'

'Sure an' you don't have to worry your head about the Frantfield Foxhounds,' Mr O'Rourke said soothingly. 'Now if it was the Old Surrey and Burstow or the West Kents, then worry you might and should. But the Frantfield Foxhounds couldn't catch a fox if it stopped to give them the time of day. They'd probably ask it to dance.'

All the same, the hunt remained at the back of Hester's mind as she prepared the basic trolley. She washed and dried her hands and put on a mask, washed the trolley down with soap and water and a Jontex cloth, then swabbed it down with 70 per cent spirits. She put the basic CSSD dressing pack on the bottom shelf and had just finished taping the used instrument bag to the end of the trolley, when she heard from faraway the sound of the hunting horn, and then Charge Nurse stood beside her, and smilingly drawled, 'Now let's take a look at how you've set up that trolley. Mr Wilkinson is ready for the fray.'

Mr Wilkinson, a retired bank manager, was as nervous as Hester. He gave her a wan smile as she wheeled her immaculately prepared trolley to his bedside. 'I am not in the least worried,' he told her. 'So please don't be afraid. I'll tell you if it hurts. But I've just spoken to Dr Lewis here and he tells me you've a gentle pair of hands.'

Peter Lewis winked. 'And steady as the proverbial rock,' he added.

The proverbial rocks were trembling a little as she cut the sealed end of the sterile pack, tipped out the inner loose end, and then snipped the adhesive holding the dressing over the wound. Once again, as she had been taught, she carefully scrubbed her hands, and returned to the next stage, opening the inner sterile pack and spreading it ready. Then came the moment she was afraid of. With sterile forceps she removed the soiled dressing and dropped it in the bag and inspected the wound. She breathed in a sigh. The wound looked healthy, but some of the stitches at the far end looked deep and indented.

She reached for the scissors and began. It was amazing how suddenly all one's mind and being could be concentrated into those tiny areas of one's eyes and fingertips, almost as though nothing else of her existed. She was dimly aware of Peter's voice, talking apparently idly to the patient, dimly aware of Charge Nurse Grant watching her intently.

But all she could see were the stitches and the tissue that surrounded them. One, two, three, four, out they came like fallen soldiers. She remembered to pull them towards the wound not away from it. Then there were two ahead deeply embedded. She wondered for a moment, cravenly, if she should ask Bill Grant to take over.

'Take your time,' a voice said steadyingly. 'You're doing fine.'

Feeling the sweat break out on her forehead, she took a deep breath. She dug carefully. Then snipped, and snipped again.

'Very good,' Charge Nurse Grant murmured.

'I positively didn't feel a thing,' Mr Wilkinson said manfully through clenched teeth, dabbing his forehead.

'D'you want to take a look as well, sir?' Peter Lewis asked respectfully, standing back.

Straightening and flicking her eyes sideways, Hester caught sight of a familiar white coat. She looked up at James Jarvis' familiar face. His expression she found withdrawn and unfamiliar.

'That was the idea, Peter,' he replied looking at Dr Lewis not at her. Then brusquely and condescendingly to Hester, 'Not bad at all, Nurse. Considering.'

'Considering what, do you suppose he meant?' Hester asked Peter Lewis.

Crossing through Casualty on her way to the carpark, she had just run into Peter, who was standing in as Casualty Officer, and he had stopped to congratulate her on her performance.

'Considering your inexperience and the relative difficulty of the job. That's my diagnosis,' Peter Lewis said. 'But does it matter? I don't suppose he meant anything. You mustn't read in things that aren't there. I don't honestly think he gave you another thought.'

'Oh,' Hester sighed, and pulled her cape

round her, feeling suddenly chilled.

'Now what have I said? Why look so de-pressed? Anyway the Boss was in a hurry, off somewhere.'

'The Hunt, no doubt,' Hester frowned. 'Escorting Miss Phillimore perhaps.'

'Ah, yes. The Hunt. We've had one patient from the Hunt in Cas. Not Miss Phillimore, thank goodness. A very portly middle-aged lady. Fractured fib. Came down in some copse. Complained they were hunting in the most impossible and unlikely terrain.'

'Did they find?'

'Find? Didn't ask, lovie. Didn't dare. Didn't want to be the bearer of bad tidings.'

Hester looked at him gratefully and he gave her a sudden tender look in return.

'I'm off in half an hour,' he said. 'How say if I get the old banger to fire on all four cylinders and come over to Honeybourne? You could give a thirsty doctor a cup of tea, couldn't you? Then we could have another look round for Broddi.'

'She's probably dead by now.'

'Rubbish!'

'And anyway we won't have much time be-fore it's dark.'

'Time enough. I could be over at your place by the time the kettle's boiled. And before you've had time to butter those sultana scones your sister makes.'

He was slightly later than he promised. The scones were buttered, and Hester had spooned out a bowl of the new season's strawberry jam, by the time he arrived.

'We had another Hunt casualty. Young chap. Not detained luckily,' Peter said apologetically. 'Just bruises. Here, let me help you with that tray. Oh, and you've lit the fire. There's a lot to be said for home comforts. Times like this I know I don't want to go on being a bachelor.' He warmed his hands at the flames.

'Did this young chap say anything about the Hunt?' Hester stared at Peter intently.

He stared into the fire and said nothing.

'I'd rather know. We've got to find out some time.'

'He said he thought they'd *found* as they say. But they hadn't killed. Not by the time he came his cropper and departed for Cas.'

'Oh.'

'And all in all he was inclined to think they wouldn't. Wouldn't kill.'

'Why?' Hester looked up from her pouring.

'Well, because foxes are crafty creatures. They double back. They go to ground. They can look after themselves.'

'Some can't.' She handed him his cup. 'Half-tame ones like Broddi can't.'

'Hester, you're an awful girl for jumping to conclusions. It probably wasn't young Broddi.

And like Mick O'Rourke said, the Frantfield Foxhounds are the bottom of the Hunt league. They've killed fewer foxes in the area than vans and motorcars. Less even than pedal bikes, I shouldn't wonder.'

Hester said miserably, 'I rather wish Broddi *had* been killed by that van.'

'Oh, my dear girl,' it seemed natural for him to come over and sit on the arm of her chair and pull her head onto his shoulder. He stroked her hair comfortingly. Her left ear was pressed against his chest. She could hear his heart beating loudly and rapidly. So loudly and rapidly that, at first, she didn't hear another sound. Then the sound did finally impinge on her consciousness, she sat suddenly bolt upright, listening.

'What's up, lovie?' Peter asked in consternation, as she pushed away his arm, 'Didn't do anything out of turn, did I?'

'Sssh.' She put her finger to her lips. Her eyes wide. It was a trick of her imagination. A mirage. Then she heard the faint scratching again, followed by a low whine. Hurling herself out of the chair and to the front door, she threw it wide open.

A damp grey and red-brown form with a long bushy white-tipped tail slithered over the threshold. It had its body low to the ground. It stopped dead in its tracks, its thick guard hairs bristling as it saw Peter, its bright green eyes gleaming in terror. Then, deciding to risk him, Broddi made a wide detour past Peter, through the open door to the kitchen and flopped exhausted in her basket by the stove.

Now it seemed natural for Hester to fling her arms round Peter in jubilation and relief. It seemed natural for him to hug her to him, for his mouth to find hers. She returned his kisses with unaccustomed abandon. All the worry over Broddi, all the suspense of the assessment, all the painful emotional contradictions came out in wild though unsophisticated kisses. When she tried to wriggle from his grasp, she knew she didn't wriggle as hard as she might.

'Darling,' Peter began thickly. But some other voice seemed to take over.

'I found the front door open,' the voice announced icily. Peter released his grip with the suddenness of a lock springing open. James Jarvis stood just inside the small sitting-room, his face pale with anger, his jaw tight, his eyes narrow. Those eyes held Hester's for several seconds. Then they went past her to the bedraggled fox just inside the kitchen. 'I am glad to see,' he said tersely, 'that she, at least, has learned her lesson.'

CHAPTER THIRTEEN

BUT THE fox had no more learned her lesson than Hester had. Twice in the following week, she managed to slip out, once when Caroline was sweeping out the patio, and once when the vicar called about distributing the offerings from the Harvest Festival. But both times, she returned home by nightfall, scratching on the door to be let in, and making low whining noises again.

'It's high time she was put back into the wild,' James Jarvis told Hester, meeting her on the staircase up to Bonnington, and pausing to enquire briefly about Broddi.

'Oh, I know what James thinks,' Caroline smiled when Hester told her over supper that evening. 'But Alistair thinks otherwise. He reckons that with a lame leg, Broddi would starve this winter. Maybe in the Spring, if we can keep her till then. And talking of the Spring . . .' her mouth softened, and averting her gaze, she stared into the fire. '. . . how would you feel, Hester, if sometime next year, say, in the Spring, I were to get married?'

She looked up suddenly and questioningly, as if she wanted to surprise her unguarded expression, as if, indeed, she suspected the strange contradictions that twisted Hester's heart. 'Oh, there's nothing definite yet, of course. But I wondered how you would feel?'

'I'd be delighted,' Hester smiled brightly. 'Really delighted. I can't think of anything that would please me more.'

'And if I were to get married,' Caroline went on, 'and please, for the moment, forget I ever mentioned it, you know that you always have a home with us. We're both so fond of you. Besides,' she laughed, 'you brought us together.'

'So I did,' Hester said steadily.

Her sister stood up, smiling as if relieved to have got a difficult emotional moment over. 'Mind if I leave the washing up? I've promised to collect some crocheting for the Church bazaar from Mrs Smith. She's an old patient of James's. And the crocheting he reckons keeps her fingers supple.' She said his name with that special inflection reserved for the object of one's affections.

'James can be very kind,' Hester said guessing some enthusiasm was required of her.

She had guessed right. 'Oh, darling!' Caroline beamed. 'I'm so pleased to hear you say that. Do you really like him?'

'Enormously,' Hester said, swallowing an uncomfortable constriction in her throat.

'I'm so glad.' Her sister buttoned up her

coat, and waved as light-heartedly as a young girl. 'Oh, and in case I don't see you before my day off on Thursday, I'm going up to town.'

'Celebration shopping?'

'A bit early for that. But I thought a new outfit might be called for.' She closed the front door behind her, opened it again briefly to say, 'I can't tell you how pleased I am you like James.'

Hester sat for a long time staring into the fire. She was hardly aware that she was crying until she felt the tears dribbling down the side of her cheeks, and onto her collar. She scrubbed them off automatically with her handkerchief and then went on staring into the fire. How could she have been so stupid, she asked herself, as to fall in love with the man her sister was to marry? Or was falling in love with James Jarvis all illusion?

Mechanically, she washed the dishes, fed Broddi, set breakfast for the morning, checked her clean white uniform dress, cleaned her black shoes and went to bed early. The following day she was on late shift. Her sister had left by the time she woke.

James Jarvis was operating that day. There were four hip replacements to prepare for Theatre. Hester's mind was therapeutically occupied. The shift flashed by. In no time they were settling the patients for the night. Mr O'Rourke was sipping his hot Ovaltine, and asking why she had hardly spared him a moment to give him the time of day, and left him to the tender mercy of the part-time SEN.

Hester was in no hurry to leave even when the night staff had taken over. She was reluctant to get back to the cottage and perhaps discuss the future with her sister. She was afraid Caroline would guess how she felt about James, or how she thought she felt about James.

But her sister was already in bed. There was a note on the kitchen table, 'Shall be leaving for London at the crack of dawn. May do a show so don't expect me till the last train. Am not on call till Fri noon.'

James Jarvis was probably also travelling up to town. He was not in hospital the following morning. Peter Lewis did a brief round. 'I thought you were on day off?' he said to Hester, helping himself to a biscuit from Sister's coffee tray, and then not listening to her reply. 'Half day. I finish at one.'

Eagerly Peter went on, 'You'll never guess who I had a card from today? Leonie Mirfield. She hates it out in Saudi. She's trying to get a job back here at home.'

Like her sister, Peter enunciated that name with the special tender emphasis of someone in love. Hester was pondering on that inflection with distant envy as she crossed the carpark to unchain her bicycle. She looked up. An ambulance was tearing past the lodge towards Casualty, its light blipping, its klaxon sounding. She paused for a moment, wondering who was inside.

It was several hours before she found out. She had returned to the cottage, washed her hair and had just finished ironing the last of her uniform dresses when the front door bell sounded. Hester glanced at the clock on the kitchen wall. Just after nine. Her sister had probably forgotten her key or Alistair was looking in to see how Broddi fared.

It was someone familiar, she decided. Broddi remained asleep in her basket. 'Just coming,' she called, pausing to shut the kitchen door behind her, lest Broddi's sleep was feigned, and hurrying to the front door, threw it open.

The light from the hall clearly illuminated the tall figure on the doorstep. But surprise made Hester peer at him as though he were a ghost.

'Mr Jarvis!' she exclaimed, finding a rather hoarse voice. 'I didn't expect . . . I mean I don't think Caroline expected, did she . . . ?' Hester's voice trailed. Something in his expression, something in his whole manner made her heart race, but whether with pleasure or fear or both, she didn't know.

'Perhaps, if I might come in?' she heard him

ask, and immediately she stepped back.

'Of course,' she murmured apologetically. 'Please do.'

'I'm sorry to come round at this time of night,' Mr Jarvis said, and then with an almost automatic return to his usual chiding manner towards her, 'I hope you're not in the habit of opening the door at night to strangers?'

She shook her head. Without thinking, she said, 'You're not a stranger.'

'Thank you.' He gave a wan and wistful smile. 'But I *might* have been. You should ask who it is before you open it.'

'I'm sorry, but I thought Caroline had forgotten her key,' Hester said, wondering why he so often managed to make her apologise. She waved him to a chair by the fire.

But he remained standing, looking down at her with a strange baffling expression in his eyes.

'She probably won't be very long. It was my sister you wanted to see, wasn't it?' Then, as he nodded, she blushed at the manifest stupidity of such a question. Who else could he possibly have come to see? Hester's wits were working slowly. Why had he come? Presumably because Caroline had at some time invited him. In that case why had Caroline not mentioned it? And why did she, Hester, feel she had some reason to cover up for her sister?

'May I get you a drink? Or some coffee? I

made some just before you came.'

He nodded. 'Thank you. Black please.'

Another thought had occurred to Hester. Perhaps her sister had invited him for supper, and in the general excitement of the possible engagement, most atypically forgotten. 'And something to eat?' she asked him.

'Just the coffee, thank you.' Hester could feel his eyes on her as she walked through into the kitchen. Then she was aware that he had followed her through and was leaning on the jamb of the doorway between the sittingroom and the kitchen, staring at her with that odd enigmatic expression on his face.

'What time do you expect Caroline to come home?' he asked her after a moment.

'The last train. That gets into Frantfield about eleven-thirty. She's left her car in the station carpark.'

'So it's about a twenty-minute drive. She should be home about midnight?'

'Yes.'

He smiled faintly like someone cracking a joke under difficult circumstances. 'Or, knowing the way Caroline drives, five minutes to.'

Hester smiled dutifully in return.

He held out his hands to take the tray of coffee from her. She hoped he didn't notice that her own hands trembled so much that the cups chimed against each other. 'Where shall I put it, Hester?'

She drew up a small oval table in front of the fire and James set the tray down carefully and looked at her with a strangely sweet and gentle smile, waiting patiently till she had settled herself in her chair, and then sitting himself down opposite her. The firelight flickered on his face, shadowing the hollows beneath his high cheekbones, softening his austere expression into something like tenderness.

It was all so domestic and intimate that just for a moment she wanted to allow herself to pretend. To pretend that he'd come to see her and not Caroline. That he had asked her not Caroline to marry him, that young as she was life wasn't after all going to be unhappy ever after.

But the pretence could only last a moment. He was clearly worried, clearly on edge, and impatient for Caroline's return.

'D'you mind if I wait till Caroline returns?' he asked suddenly in an oddly quiet and humble voice for such an autocratic man.

Did she mind? Hester thought with a wild leap of her heart. Did she mind having the man she loved to herself for the next two and a half hours? Surely he must be blind not to see how little she minded.

'Of course not.'

'You weren't wanting an early night or anything were you?'

'Me? Oh, no.'

'Because if you are, just carry on. I'll read the paper, or watch the television.' He smiled wryly. 'You don't have to stay up to entertain me. Just go to bed.'

'I'm not at all tired.'

'Only,' he went on as if she hadn't spoken, 'it *is* rather important that I see her tonight.' He drank the coffee Hester handed him in silence and then put down the cup and, leaning across, picked up her hand. He held it tenderly as if for one delirious, deluded moment he really cared about her, Hester. Then he said, 'Perhaps you'll be able to help me put this to her.'

Hester's hand seemed to stiffen in his grasp. 'Put what?' she asked hoarsely. 'A proposal?'

He frowned, and shook his head impatiently. 'It's about someone of whom she's very fond.'

'You?' she quavered.

'No,' his frown deepened. 'Of course not. Please don't interrupt. It's about Alistair Matherson. He was attacked by the bull over at Yates' farm and badly gored. He was brought in several hours ago.'

'I'm sorry,' he said quickly. His grip on her hand tightened. 'This is a shock for you too. I know you're fond of him as well. But obviously not as she is.'

Hester hardly heard him. Her mind went back to the ambulance with its klaxon sounding. 'Is he badly hurt?'

He paused. 'Yes.' Coolly, dispassionately, he told her. The clinical detail was momentarily therapeutic. He spoke in a deliberate clipped, precise voice. The fractures were not a problem, but internal injuries . . . He was in Intensive Care. As a widower he had no near relatives and had given Caroline as his next-of-kin.

With the strange distorting effect of shock, time telescoped and expanded. Hester seemed to have been sitting in front of the fire for hours, with James staring at her in an oddly intent manner, as if she were the patient and not poor Alistair. The next moment the phone was ringing and as if it had jerked a puppet on a string, Hester leapt to her feet and snatched up the receiver.

Someone was calling from a phone box. Hester heard the peeps and then her sister's voice, 'Oh, Hester. Thank goodness I got you. Can't stop. No more coins. Listen, the last train's been cancelled. I'll get into a hotel somewhere. Are you sure you'll be all right on your own . . . ?'

And then as Hester found her voice and spoke urgently into the receiver, 'Caroline, wait! Please! Hang on . . . I've something to tell you.'

The pips sounded, the phone went dead.

'I'm sorry,' Hester turned to James, as he came across the room, hand outstretched, to take the phone. 'I made a mess of that. I didn't realise . . . I should have . . . my mind just doesn't seem to be functioning.'

She put her hand to her head. She felt the skin of her forehead break out in a cold sweat, as the stupefying effect of immediate shock wore off. The room spun round her. She felt herself falling down and down into darkness. But the darkness was without terror, for a pair of warm strong arms had caught and held her in it.

CHAPTER FOURTEEN

HESTER opened her eyes to find herself still in those comfortable supporting arms. Her head rested against his chest and she could feel his breath on her hair. Her feet swung loosely as they moved . . . across a room? No, climbing. The toe of her shoe just touched the side of the staircase and he shifted her weight protectively away.

He must have been scrutinising her face, and seen the flutter of her eyelids.

'Feeling better?' He sounded distant and unemotional.

'Much better. Thank you. Sorry. It was silly of me. You can put me down now.' She looked up sideways at him. In the shadowy staircase light his expression was unreadable. She tried to push herself away from him but his grip tightened.

'I'm putting you to bed,' he said tersely, 'Which is your room?'

'The one on the right at the top of the stairs,' she said in a still, small voice. And in an even smaller voice, 'I'm sorry to be such a nuisance. I should have been a help and . . .' Her voice trailed away, as he gave her a little squeeze of mingled comfort and exasperation.

'Don't be silly,' he said sharply. 'There's nothing to be sorry for.'

He stood on the small landing. The pink-shaded light almost brushed his head. It threw their joined shadows on the white landing wall.

'Now, is this your room?'

The door was ajar. He nudged it further open.

'Can you turn on the light, Hester? You know where the switch is.'

With the light directly on her, just before he set her carefully on the bed, he scrutinised her face. His eyes were narrow, his mouth oddly tight.

'Kick off your shoes,' he said, standing over her. 'Stretch out. Now,' he perched himself on the bed beside her, and picked up her wrist in his long cool fingers. Her heart she knew was beating rapidly and erratically in an uncomfortable mixture of ecstasy and misery. He held his fingers on her pulse for what seemed too short and too long a time, frowning at his wrist watch. Then he sighed, and touched her cheek with his forefinger as if to coax some colour into it.

'Feel able to get yourself into bed?'

She nodded, then added, 'But I don't want to go to bed.'

He put his finger on her lips, and said quite nicely but with an edge of impatience, 'Do as you're told, Hester. Please don't argue.'

'You could meet the first train into Frantfield Wells,' Hester suggested, 'Caroline will be on that. It gets in about seven.'

He inclined his head. 'I could.'

'Shall you?'

'Perhaps.'

It dawned on her that now she was no more than a nuisance to him, a hindrance, when he had hoped for her help.

'Would you like a hot drink?' he asked her, confirming it. 'I've no doubt I could find my way round Caroline's kitchen,' again Hester heard that slight tender inflection at the mention of Caroline's name.

'No, thank you.'

'I'll say goodnight then,' he patted her shoulder. It was all she could do not to catch that hand and press it to her lips.

Instead she said, 'It's a Yale latch on the front door. If you pull it to after you.'

'Thank you,' he gave her a brief nod, turned in the doorway to give her one last quick scrutiny, and then closed her bedroom door softly behind him.

She undressed quickly and clambered into bed. She felt suddenly overwhelmed with tiredness, as if not just the residue of the last few hours, but of days and weeks and months, had suddenly caught up with her.

For a while, she listened for the click of the

front door. Once the click of a door seemed to penetrate her dreams. They were wild, distorted nightmare dreams. Clare Phillimore and James Jarvis riding to hounds, with Caroline rushing in tears after them. They had found and killed, for in her dreams she heard the terrible scream of a vixen and then silence. Someone came into the dream in a car and somewhere there was the ringing of a telephone, and voices, laughing voices, and doors clicking again.

Hester woke to the smell of coffee, which was strange in an empty house. With the resilience of youth, she felt fit and rested and hungry. Then the awful thought struck her that she had overslept. She couldn't, for a moment, remember whether she was on early or late duty. Though her body felt refreshed, her mind still felt as if it was filled with cotton wool.

She looked at the calendar on the bedside table. She was on late duty. She looked at her bedside clock. Seven forty-five. Her sister's train would be already in. James Jarvis would presumably have met her. Now the full memory of last night flooded in.

But why the smell of coffee? And why distant voices? Hester threw back the bedclothes, pulled on her dressing-gown and tiptoed downstairs.

Half way down, she saw that the door from the tiny hall to the sittingroom was open. She saw Caroline was already back. James was with her. They were standing just by the telephone. James was slowly replacing the receiver.

He suddenly put up his thumb and gave her one of his rare tender smiles, and without a word spoken Hester saw Caroline throw herself into his arms.

Explanations of a somewhat surprising sort came later. Having retreated to her room to lick her wounds, Hester tried to force herself to accept what she had seen. It was, after all, what she had wanted. Once, more than anything else in the world. Why now, did it so distress her? Why did the realisation almost force her to forget about Alistair, and how he was, and what his special relationship, if any, to Caroline might be?

Unable to find the explanations herself, Hester bathed and dressed carefully. Then, only when she had heard the opening of the front door and looking out seen James's lithe form striding down the path to the gate, did she re-emerge.

Caroline was in the kitchen, humming as she restocked her surgical bag. She looked up and smiled radiantly at Hester.

'Darling,' she came over and gave Hester a peck on her cheek. 'Are you OK? James and I had a peep at you when I arrived back and you seemed fine.'

Hester nodded. Then she asked, 'How's Alistair?'

'So far, so good. James has just spoken to the hospital. Alistair had a comfortable night. James says I'll be allowed to go in to see him tomorrow.'

'Did James meet you from the train?'

'No,' her sister shook her head. 'He waited till I got home here.'

'Waited?' Hester exclaimed. *'Here? All night?'*

'Yes, darling. He waited all night. Don't sound so shocked and scandalised. It's I who should sound both.' She smiled. 'What would the neighbours think?' Her smile deepened into laughter at Hester's bewildered expression.

'I didn't mean that,' Hester said. 'I meant he knew you weren't coming home. And it was you he came to see. So why did he wait?'

'So that you weren't alone. Especially when you weren't well. He was concerned about you.'

'Oh,' Hester said with a long sigh.

'He also kept in touch with the hospital. He got the latest on Alistair. So when I got back he had both bad and good news for me.'

'That was kind.'

'Poor old you,' Caroline squeezed Hester's hand, 'you took the brunt.'

'There wasn't much brunt,' Hester smiled

determinedly. 'I don't deserve any sympathy.' Last night had been like a small delicious taste of some forbidden fruit, she thought, but not aloud.

A silence full of unasked and unanswered questions seemed to fall between them. Then Caroline glanced at the kitchen clock and snapped her bag shut as if the time for asking questions was up.

Desperately, Hester tried to form the difficult words. 'Tell me,' she asked thickly, 'Are you in love with him?'

'Yes,' her sister answered simply and patted her shoulder in the way James Jarvis had done.

'If anyone were to tell me,' Sister Bonnington said later that week, 'that a more obstreperous patient could ever be found than Mr O'Rourke, I would certainly have said he was pulling my leg. But from what I hear from IC about the vet who was gored by a bull, I might be wrong.'

Sister was speaking more in sorrow than in anger, because she had been balked of giving a challenging case like Alistair's her famed and special treatment. Alistair, having made remarkable progress in Intensive Care, had insisted on being moved to a small private clinic near his veterinary hospital, so that his veterinary nurses and assistant could come in and be instructed on how to treat his patients.

'I saw your friend the vet,' Peter Lewis told Hester at tea-time as he scrounged a left-over piece of sponge cake, 'in IC. He's got great faith in your sister. He told me that in no time he would discharge himself from the clinic, and have your sister look in on him at home.'

Certainly the vet's faith in Caroline was not found to be misplaced. Caroline seemed hardly ever to be at the cottage. When she wasn't nursing Alistair she was no doubt with James. In fact, at first, Hester thought that the strange behaviour of the fox cub was because it was moping at being left too much on its own. It looked listless, and even when the back door was left open, made no attempt to escape. But as the days went by, and October gave way to the chilly mists of November the fox seemed unmistakably ill.

'I don't think I ought to mention it to Alistair at the moment,' Caroline said over a snatched breakfast together. 'I spend half my time stopping him giving distant diagnoses. I'm not going to give him one iota to do that I can stop him doing.'

'We could send for another vet,' Hester suggested.

But Caroline seemed reluctant, almost as if it were disloyal so to do. 'Broddi's rather his baby. Let's see how she is towards the end of the week.'

But the end of the week brought no improvement, at least not for Broddi. There was much improvement to the patients on Bonnington. Mr Wilkinson had gone home. There was talk of Kenny and Johnny and even Mr O'Rourke being discharged. There was also talk on the hospital grapevine that Miss Phillimore was getting married, marquees had been ordered, an enormous wedding was planned. And on Friday early shift, as they made beds together, Sheila Richardson told Hester she'd heard the bridegroom was none other than Mr Jarvis.

Late home as her sister was that night, Hester sat up for her. It was as if their respective roles were reversed.

She was about to tax her with an unequivocal question, 'Just who is it that you're in love with? And if it's James Jarvis, why this gossip? Why does he see so much of Clare Phillimore? Aren't you afraid that he may treat you the same way again?'

But there was really no need to ask. In the early hours a car drew up. The front door softly opened and there was Caroline and her escort. Her sister had changed out of her uniform and was wearing a lovely green velvet suit with a frothy white blouse underneath. She was radiant and starry-eyed. She was accompanied by James Jarvis. He was immaculate and handsome in dinner jacket. A handsome pair in fact, Hester thought, and tried to make that thought without envy.

'Hester, my dear,' Caroline said concerned-ly, as they shut the front door behind them. 'You look worried. Is something wrong? Is Broddi worse? Or are *you* not well?'

From behind her sister James eyed her close-ly and with sudden older brother's concern.

'No,' Hester said stonily. 'Not exactly. She's eating quite well. But I think there *is* some-thing very wrong.' She was unsure now how to explain herself. But no explanations were necessary.

James suddenly shouldered his way out of his dinner jacket and rolled up his white shirt sleeves. He gave them both one of his rare sweet smiles. 'Well, let *me* take a look. I won't be a patch on Alistair. But I'm beginning to get the hang of foxy anatomy. And at least I'm someone Broddi knows.'

'That's why he came,' Caroline said as though in answer to some unspoken objection from Hester. 'We both went to see Alistair and then out to dinner.' She took James's jacket from him and hung it up, watching him walk through to the kitchen, and stand over the fox's basket.

'Right, my girl.' He let the vixen smell his hand. 'Take your time. You remember me. Now I'm not going to hurt you.' Gently, James squatted down beside Broddi. Gently he stroked the vixen's fur. Then gently he turned her over and ran his hands slowly over her body. 'No. Don't wriggle. Here! Hester! Caroline! Hold her a moment, one of you. One more minute. Hold her back legs. I just want to be sure.' Obediently, Hester did as he told her, her eyes on his face. Her cheek brushed his, but he didn't seem to notice.

'Thanks. That'll do.' He straightened, walked over to the kitchen sink and washed his hands. He was smiling to himself.

'Don't look so worried,' he told them both. 'It's perfectly natural, as our gynae friends would say. She's not ill. Your family is about to increase. She's in cub.' He put his arms round both their shoulders, and hugged them to him in an oddly boyish and oddly endearing gesture. 'Now what exactly are you going to do about *that*?'

Broddi decided what exactly should be done.

Three days later, lulled by the fact that Broddi never seemed to want to escape, Caroline left the back door open while she swept the kitchen doorstep, and in a flash Broddi was gone.

'She'll be back,' Caroline said at first. 'She'll do as she did last time. As soon as she's hungry, she'll scratch at the door.'

But she didn't. And now the hunting season was in full swing. Even Mr O'Rourke seemed less confident, and less decisive about the Frantfield Foxhounds. For they had already killed twice, and a lame vixen, heavy in cub, with no mate to divert the hounds from her, wouldn't stand any sort of chance.

'I'll help you look for her again,' Peter Lewis said. 'Count on me for my next half day. I'll be there I promise.'

But when his half day came, so also did news of Leonie Mirfield. She was back from Saudi. The hospital were to give her a temporary post at the Day Hospital. And Hester was to guess what, she'd asked him and only him to help her look for a little bed-sitter in Frantfield Wells. So would Hester mind if they postponed the search for Broddi? In any case he'd heard that a hunt was scheduled that afternoon, so it wouldn't be the best time to wander round trying to find a stray fox.

'My pals tell me that there are some foxes' earths in the woods beyond the quarries,' Mr O'Rourke told Hester just before she finished her half day duty. 'She might seek out her own kind again. But watch it. The Hunt know about the earths too. An' if I know them they'll have been after stopping up those earths.'

'Alistair says it's useless to try to find her.' Caroline was home for lunch. She was in the kitchen preparing a salad. 'Now she's in cub, we must let her go.'

'He's come round to James's way of thinking?'

'Now he has. Because circumstances have

changed.' She gave Hester her oddly lit-up smile.

'You love James very much, don't you?' Hester said mistily.

'James?' her sister looked astonished. 'Yes, I think I do,' she replied slowly after a moment. 'I'm certainly very fond of him. But it's Alistair I'm in love with, darling. Alistair I'm going to marry. That's why I was so grateful you found Broddi and brought us together. Why are you looking at me like that? You weren't in any doubt that it was Alistair, were you? Did you think . . . James and I? Oh, my dear girl! Just because I knew him? Because he's an old friend.'

'You were in love with him before!'

'Never. I was never in love with James. Nor he with me.'

'Marigold . . .'

'Marigold always was a romantic.'

'She said he left you in the lurch. And that was why you never married.'

'James and I were friends. And *nothing* else. Oh, I know everyone thought I must have had an unhappy love affair just because I didn't marry. That I must have given up someone simply to look after you. But, believe it or not, I never wanted to marry till I really fell in love. It's hard for people to understand that some-times. They think everyone should be married by a certain age. But I never fell in love till I met Alistair. Do *you* understand?'

Hester shook her head.

'I told you I love James, yes. As an old friend. It would be hard to know James and not love him. I think you might say,' she went on slowly, 'that I love him like a brother.'

'But James . . .'

'But nothing. James isn't in love with me. He never was. After my party he went abroad. I didn't see him again till he came back here with you. James . . .' she drew a deep breath.

'I think I know what you're going to say,' Hester protested. Suddenly she'd guessed and she knew she didn't want to hear her sister say it. 'James is in love,' she said harshly. 'That's what you were trying to say, isn't it?'

'Far be it from me to say it. I shouldn't. I *mustn't*. But if you insist, yes that's really what you should know.'

'Not with you, Caroline? But with *someone else*.'

Her sister nodded, her eyes averted. 'I thought you'd have guessed, my dear,' she said gently. 'Surely you have?'

Hester didn't reply. Without another word she turned on her heel. The kitchen, the whole cottage suddenly seemed suffocating. She had to escape. Somehow it wouldn't have been so bad if James and Caroline had been in love. But James and Miss Phillimore was more than she could bear.

On impulse, she went round to the shed and wheeled out her bicycle, and without thinking sped down the High Street and then turned on the little cross country road that led to the quarries and the Downs.

CHAPTER FIFTEEN

THE COOL autumn air and her own speed were oddly therapeutic. Hester found she could take a more rational, even if it was a more melancholy view of what had happened. At least her sister was in love with a good, loving dependable man who returned her love. In the fullness of time, she, Hester, might also find someone to love her. She would know, of course, that she couldn't, like Caroline, wait for the right man to come along. Because the right man had already come into her life. And gone.

Reaching the swell of the Downs behind the quarries, Hester rested her bicycle against a tree stump and began to walk up the soft springy slippery turf that covered the chalky ground. Intermittently, as she walked towards the quarries and the woods beyond, she called. But there was no answer except the rustling of the few dead leaves on the wind-bent trees.

That there were foxes, however, somewhere near was obvious from their peculiar musky scent. It hung in the little hollows between the gaping hillside holes, where stone and chalk had been quarried it was said since Roman times.

It also became obvious that, as Mr O'Rourke had told her, the Hunt too knew of the foxes' earths, and that the scent was being carried to more predatory nostrils than hers. For distantly, at first, and then nearer, came the sound of a hunting horn. Followed a minute or two later by the yapping of fox hounds.

Hester was just walking along the southern lip of the largest quarry, a great carved-out pit whose distant bottom was filled with deep blue water, when a movement caught her eye on the other side. A fox disturbed by the sound of the horn had broken cover from the woods beyond. It was moving swiftly but with a pronounced limp.

'Broddi!' Hester shrieked, and simultaneously over the hill behind her, came the hounds in full cry. She could see the moving dots of them on the horizon, their sterns waving. Then the figures of the huntsmen, the crack of a whip and the whole pack spreading out as if cutting off all retreat.

The fox froze into total immobility. Then, to Hester's horror, she saw the vixen try to pick her way over the lip of the quarry and down the inside, as if it might lead eventually to some safe earth.

'No!' Hester shouted, racing round the jagged edge of the quarry, sending scatterings of kicked-up chalk skeltering over the edge to plop long after in the water below. 'No! Don't!

They'll corner you there. You'll be trapped.'
But poor foolish Broddi was slipping and sliding down the sheer face, while Hester ran in
panic, her eyes darting from the approaching
hounds to the vixen. All she could think of was
that soon she would see Broddi torn bloodily to
pieces before her. Her mind was filled with that
vision. She tried to run faster treading closer to
the crumbling edge.

Suddenly she slipped sideways on the turf.
The lip of the quarry gave under her feet and
she was over the edge.

The quarry was deep and full of jagged
outcrops. Hester kept putting out her hands to
try to grab one, sharp though they were. Anything to stop her sliding towards that sinister
blue water at the deepest. Rocks skinned her
hands, ripped her nails, bruised her head.

All at once with a hard bump she stopped
dead. Her fall had been broken by a rocky
ledge, to which she now clung with the strength
of desperation.

She seemed to have been plunging downwards for a lifetime, but it could only have been
a matter of seconds. She had descended half
way down the quarry. About twenty yards
away, but well above her, Broddi had also
found a resting place in a shallow indentation
where once a fallen boulder must have rested.
The vixen was shivering in panic as the sound
of the hounds came nearer, and distantly vi-

brating through the ground came the drum of horses' hoofs.

In those few seconds as she assessed the scene, Hester felt she'd touched the bottom of despair. Nothing and no one could save Broddi now. No one could save her witnessing the vixen's terrible end. For the hundredth time she wished she had never found Broddi, never taken her home, never looked after her.

Then, looking up on the lip of the quarry, Hester seemed to see a mirage. A huge dog fox half as big again as the vixen had appeared. He seemed to be looking, as Hester had done, from the trembling vixen in the quarry, to the seemingly inescapable spread of the pack of approaching hounds.

For what seemed far too long a time, he simply stood there motionless against the skyline, clearly visible to the surrounding countryside. Then there was a furious blaring of the horn as the MFH gave the signal for *Found*. It seemed to have been the very signal the huge fox had been listening and waiting for. Immediately he heard it he was off. At first, Hester thought he was running for his life and deserting the vixen. Then she realised that like the Pied Piper all the hounds and horses were being drawn after him.

For a time, the quarry seemed to vibrate to the sound of retreating hoofs, to shouts and orders, the crack of the whipper-in, the notes of the horn and the baying of the hounds. Gradually they all faded.

Then there was silence. The quarry held a terrible cup of shadowy quiet. Above them the Downland was empty of people. Somewhere in the woods a missel thrush sang. Broddi gave a little whine. Then the quarry lapsed into silence again. Suddenly Hester noticed that the sun was going down, and for the first time she began to be afraid, not only for Broddi but also for herself.

She began by calling, softly at first and then with ever increasing desperation. What if no one came to look for her? What if the ledge she crouched on gave way?

She could no longer see the deep pool at the bottom of the quarry because it was hidden in shadow that seemed to creep up towards her, like the water itself.

She tried not to think about what might happen. She tried not to think about the stiffness of her limbs. She found the only antidote was to think about James.

At first, her thoughts began as a melancholy musing on their times together. She had often heard that in danger of death one's whole life flashed before one. And James was in a way her life. Only suddenly the events didn't take place as she had thought they had done. They took a different, beguilingly happy meaning.

If James didn't, wasn't in love with Caroline, why had he been so delighted to come to the cottage? And why was he so protective, stern yes, but protective and thoughtful? And why had Caroline been so happy that she, Hester, liked James? Why had she, Hester, jumped to the conclusion that he was in love with Clare Phillimore? Just because of seeing them a few times together and because of hospital gossip? Why should the notoriously inaccurate hospital grapevine in general and the even more inaccurate Sheila, in particular, get the gossip right this time? Why had Caroline said it was not her place to say who James was in love with, (as indeed it wasn't) and yet look so lovingly delighted about it? If it *wasn't* Hester? Had Caroline realised Hester was in love with James long before she herself had realised it?

At the thought of that possibility, however remote, Hester began calling again with renewed strength.

The quarry, she had discovered, had a strange echo. Her voice went round and round in ever diminishing circles till it died away to a breathy whisper. Occasionally this whisper was made even more despairing by Broddi's shrill whine.

Then, just as she was beginning to feel the grip of icy terror again, her voice came back to her, not in an ever fading echo, but in a man's deep call.

'Hester? Where are you?' A man's head and shoulders appeared black against the sky above the lip of the quarry, and there was James.

She lifted one hand to him, and immediately he said sharply, 'Don't do that. Don't move. Hold on a moment. I'm coming down.'

She heard the sound of a hammer on a steel peg, then she saw the figure of James testing the rope against the rock. Minutes later he was skimming down the side of the quarry towards her, his body looming large and powerful and solid in the shadow of the quarry.

She felt his arms go round her, and then the most enchanting words she had ever heard, 'Are you all right, my darling?'

She nodded speechlessly. It was as if she was afraid to speak and break the dream. 'Now,' he said, speaking softly, 'I'm going to tie this round you, so we can get you up safely.'

He put the rope round her waist. 'It's lucky,' he said softly, 'that I know a little about climbing.' Then, half dragging, half walking her, he hoisted her up the side.

They both collapsed on the turf at the top, side by side, letting out long sighs of relief, then wordlessly moving into each others arms and holding the other tightly, without speaking and without kissing. Just holding.

'Now, my darling.' Reluctantly he released

her and knelt beside her. 'Let's take a good look at you.'

He smiled ruefully, as if apologising for the doctor taking over from the man. He looked into her eyes, then slowly ran his hands over her body.

'Is that painful, my dear?' he asked, smiling commiseratingly as he lightly touched the sore place on her forehead. 'But no bones broken as far as I can tell. You're lucky,' he looked at her meaningfully, 'we're both lucky, aren't we?'

'Oh, James!' She lifted her arms to him and when he bent over her, she fastened them round his neck. 'I didn't know till now how lucky I was. How lucky I am. That is if you . . .'

'I do,' he bent closer still, and brushed her lips with his. 'I do love you. I shall always love you.' He put his fingers under her chin, and kissed her lips with a curious firm tenderness. Behind that tenderness she could sense a passion carefully controlled, as if even now he was determined to play fair with her. His next words confirmed it. 'But you're still very young, and I'm . . .'

'Exactly the right age, and I love you.' She felt suddenly very mature.

He laughed. 'I find it very hard to believe that you do. It's been very hard not to show how much I loved you.'

Demurely she said, 'You've concealed it

very well.' And with a sideways smile, 'When did you begin to love me?'

'From the moment you spilled Mr O'Rourke's champagne. And talking of Mr O'Rourke. When Caroline phoned me at the hospital, it was O'Rourke who told me where I might find you. So I came prepared with rope and irons.'

'Dear James. Dear Mr O'Rourke,' Hester sighed. 'I'm grateful to him on several counts. He guessed I . . .'

'At first *I* thought . . . well, let's say,' James smiled as ruefully as a young boy, 'you seemed to return my interest. Then I began to discover that you wanted me for Caroline.'

'I only *thought* I did. I preferred you loved Caroline rather than Clare Phillimore. And when I heard Clare was getting married, and you . . .'

'She isn't getting married! That's just hospital gossip. The marquees are for her twenty-first party. My fiancée and I will be invited I shouldn't wonder. You owe Sir Terence a thank you anyway. He diverted the cubbing miles away from where they might get Broddi.'

'Oh,' Hester said, 'That's why you were at Frantfield Lodge that day?'

'Yes, Sir Terence and I had a little discussion. We decided that was the best solution.'

Hester sighed. 'And I told you . . .'

He smiled wryly, 'That you hated me, yes.'

Hester shook her head apologetically. 'I never knew whether I loved you or hated you.'

'Like Sister and Mr O'Rourke?'

'Oh, they hate each other!' Hester answered promptly.

'Do they now,' James mimicked Mr O'Rourke's Irish accent, 'then why was he after inviting her to some shoot in Yorkshire and why was she after prettily accepting?' James shook his head. 'I fear Sister has been got at.'

'Love and hate,' Hester shook her head, 'are very difficult to diagnose sometimes,' and in the same breath, 'have you ever loved anyone before me? Really been in love, I mean?'

'Never.'

'Caroline?'

'I was fond of her. As a friend and a colleague.'

'That was why you gave her the watch?'

'How on earth did you remember that?'

She laughed. Then she asked, 'What about Clare Phillimore? You were attentive to her?'

'I simply made up a party. But I suppose then you decided to encourage Peter Lewis? Kissed him, I remember, at that dance. And on other occasions.'

Hester sighed. 'I think I just stood-in occasionally for Leonie.'

'To my fury.'

She sat up. 'Were you jealous? Really?'

'Yes,' he said tersely and pulled her to her feet. He put his arms round her and kissed her, this time with almost punishing ardour, the passion, withheld before now lighting her own. She wondered how she could ever have thought Peter's kisses exciting. 'Now,' James said quietly, 'now you see how jealous I was. And why.'

'Tell me again,' she breathed.

For several minutes, it seemed that the world outside did not exist. Then gradually she became aware of a distant whimpering.

She spun round. She saw that the huge dog fox had returned and was now crouched on the lip of the quarry.

'I'd forgotten all about Broddi!' Hester exclaimed guiltily. 'What shall we do? How can we get her up?'

'*We*,' James said, 'don't have to do anything. Look.'

From where they stood, they saw Broddi creep out a little further from her shallow hole, making that strange little churring noise of greeting she used to make to Caroline and Hester.

The big dog fox barked in return. Then he was edging carefully down towards her in a wide curving route that took him just beyond her. He paused for a moment on a narrow ledge, whining as if to tell her to follow. Cautiously, then with gathering confidence she edged forward to him. Together they zig-zagged along what seemed to be a track well-known to the dog fox. The track brought them gradually back up towards the lip of the quarry. Both animals finally emerged not twenty yards from where Hester and James stood.

For a moment, fox and vixen stood quite still, regarding them. Then the dog fox turned away. As she prepared to follow him Broddi threw them one green-eyed glance, gave them one last affectionate churr before the pair of them loped off.

Hester watched them moving swiftly away, till they disappeared into the black shadows of the wood.

'Would you say our vixen has finally learned her lesson?' Hester asked, not sure whether to laugh or cry.

'I think we've all learned some sort of lesson,' James put his arm round her. 'Certainly she's learned where she belongs.'

He kissed her lips slowly and lingeringly. Then, slipping his arm round her shoulders, he began to walk her towards the road and his car and the faraway lights below. 'And now, it's time for me to take you home!'